In the Midst of Deceit
A Novel

Deborah M. Piccurelli

In the Midst of Deceit—A Novel
published by Jireh Publishing Company

For information:
Jireh Publishing Company
P.O. Box 4263
San Leandro, CA 94579-0263

ISBN 1-893995-25-9

To the memory of Carmela Piccurelli: my mother-in-law, friend, first reviewer, and greatest encourager. Also, to my husband whose loving support is invaluable. And most importantly, to my Lord Jesus, without whom this book would not have been possible.

PROLOGUE

HE WINCED INWARDLY AS HE MET THE DULL, BLUE EYES OF the elderly woman sitting across from him. She was tiny and frail. Her full head of silvery hair was clipped short and neatly coiffured. The sweeping skirt of her floral print dress fell over her knees in graceful folds. The woman searched the man's face, as if trying to discern his reliability and trustworthiness. Vulnerability issued from her every glance, every action, indicating she was an easy target.

As he tugged at the collar of his dress shirt, he felt the color rising up his neck. This was somebody's grandmother. She reminded him of his own grandmother, momentarily producing a slight pang of guilt for what he was about to do.

Mrs. Haloran's hand quivered as she wrote out the check, her handwriting shaky. He imagined that was a thing to be expected with old age.

"This is an awful lot of money," Mrs. Haloran remarked.

She looked worried. She should be.

He cleared his throat. "No need for concern, Mrs. Haloran. I'll take good care of it for you," he soothed. During the course of his career, he had developed a silky, comforting tone to his voice that compelled people to trust him. It worked well. Especially on lonely, elderly women.

"Are you sure it won't get lost?"

"Positive."

"It won't get into the wrong hands, will it?"

He sighed, frustrated, his fingers itching to close around that check. "Trust me, Mrs. Haloran. That money will be in good hands."

Slowly setting the pen down on the massive, glossy oak desk, she gazed at him apprehensively.

He tapped his foot beneath the desk. This was getting old—fast. Leaning forward, he looked her straight in the eye to emphasize the point of what he said next: "If you can't trust me, who *can* you trust?"

Ejecting a sigh, she relented. "Very well." Tearing off the check, she handed it to him.

The moment his eyes locked on to all those zeroes, any spark of guilt he may have felt was completely extinguished.

CHAPTER ONE

STRUGGLING WITH TWO BULGING, SLIPPING GROCERY BAGS, Stasi Courtland jabbed the key at her apartment door.

"Need some help?" came a deep, familiar voice from behind her.

"Ahh!" she cried. "I'm about to lose my eggs!"

5   He deftly plucked the bags from her arms.

"Thank you." She threw her neighbor, Slade Mitchell, a smile and unlocked the door. "You always seem to show up at just the right moment."

Slade grinned mischievously as he carried the bags to the kitchen counter. "I can always sense when a beautiful woman is in peril."

Stasi rolled her eyes. Slade could charm a snake out of a basket without the flute. The thing was, he knew it.

"Well," he said as he moved toward the door. "I'm happy to have been of service, but I have to get ready for a date. I wouldn't impress the lady looking like this."

Wouldn't he? Stasi took in his appearance: green knit gym shorts, a white muscle shirt that bore a large, cone-shaped damp spot where it clung to his broad chest. Strings of dark hair adhered to his sweat-drenched forehead. His neck and shoulders glistened with perspiration as well, evidencing his previous exertion which, she guessed, was jogging.

Oh, yes, she was reasonably sure that even in his present state he'd make a deep impression on most women—the operative word being *most*. Falling for the suave manners and superficiality of his type wasn't her style.

"Okay," she said, trying to cover up her scrutiny of him. "I appreciate your help. Have a nice time on your date."

He smiled roguishly, flashing bright, even teeth. "I have no doubt that I will." Waggling his eyebrows, he swept out of the apartment.

Shaking her head, she unpacked the groceries. Not only was he a charmer—he was conceited as all get out. She supposed it wasn't *all* his fault. Everyone idolized him and let him know it.

He had everything going for him: successful in business, well-to-do, popular (though she felt that his income and popularity were somehow connected), and good looking—with dangerously dark eyes, chiseled features, muscular shoulders, and trim waist—the ultimate personification of the cliché "tall, dark, and handsome." Women threw themselves at him and hung on his every word, as well as his person.

She'd never condone that sort of behavior. Stasi believed she was the only woman in creation who didn't swoon around Slade Mitchell. Slade knew that wasn't her style, and she felt that irked him. Used to having women trip all over themselves to be near him, he seemed to try even harder to impress Stasi and gain her attention and admiration. But he had found out from the first day she moved into Chestnut House Apartments that materialism and persona were of no importance to her.

That was four months ago. Stasi's parents had sold their home in the neighboring town of Haddon Heights and retired to Annapolis. Not wanting to leave the southern New Jersey area, Stasi decided to take an apartment in the quaint, historic town of Haddonfield. She had always loved how some of the sidewalks along Kings Highway, which ran through the center of town, were still made of cobbled brick. As one walked along this main strip lined with small, upscale shops, the aroma of fresh ground coffee or the pungent odor of a variety of cheeses stirred one's senses. Moreover, Haddonfield was a "dry town" and a place that drew elite society to reside. Hence, it would be beneficial to Stasi's growing business.

On that first day, much like today, Slade had offered to help as she struggled with a stack of heavy boxes. It hadn't seemed to bother him that he was on his way to work, impeccably dressed in a soft, gray wool suit with matching gray Italian leather shoes. His large frame cast her in shadow as he took the boxes from her. "My name is Anastasia Courtland," she said. "My friends call me Stasi."

He rolled his eyes. "Cute name."

Stasi sighed. Everyone had some kind of reaction to her name. "My mother loved the movie with Ingrid Bergman. Besides," she added defensively, "I like my name. What's yours?"

Carrying the boxes in, he looked around. "Where do you want these?"

"Oh." She glanced around. "On the dining room table."

Just about the time she'd decided he was never going to answer her question, he said, "Slade Mitchell." Strolling around the room, he picked up and examined a knickknack, a picture frame, making himself at home as if he had every right.

"Oh. And what kind of name is Slade?" she shot at him, still smarting from his earlier sarcasm.

Everything about him—his stance, his expression, even his style of dress—screamed ARROGANCE!

"I don't know. You'll have to ask my mother." Coming up beside her, he leaned close. "But it's *my* name, and *I* like it."

Touché.

At that moment, Stasi knew that this guy would somehow spell trouble for her.

Moving back to the boxes he'd placed on the table, Slade peered into the lidless box on top of the stack. Lifting out a burgundy leather-bound book, he inspected it, then stated the obvious: "This is a Bible."

Stasi glanced over briefly, then resumed the unpacking she'd started. "Uh-huh."

"Do you . . . read it?"

"All the time."

Scratching his head, he stood staring at it as though it were some sort of UFO.

Stasi walked over, gently took the Book from him, and, hugging it to her chest, said, "I live by this Book."

She watched the perplexed expression he wore morph into one of apprehension and could almost hear the "uh-oh" ringing through his mind like an alarm.

After making excuses about getting to work, Slade made a hasty exit.

Now, as she finished putting the groceries away, she thought: *He really isn't the sort of person I want to socialize with, anyway. More important, he's not a believer.*

By the end of the first month in her new apartment, Stasi found out he lived life in the fast lane. She could hear parties going on across the hall at all hours, every weekend. Many times, late at night, she heard giggling and hushed murmurs in the hall, indicating he'd brought a woman home to spend the night.

So even though she had to admit that he was attractive, she could never be attracted *to* him.

But if he were to ever change . . .

CHAPTER TWO

SLADE WAS LATE FOR WORK AGAIN. IT DIDN'T MATTER, though. One of the perks of being in a partnership was that you could do almost anything you wanted and nobody could give you a set down. Besides, he generated plenty of business, so his partners couldn't complain.

Zipping into the reserved parking space in front of the office building on prestigious Main Street, he emerged from his brand-new silver Jaguar. He was proud of *that* baby. That was another advantage of owning a business: making enough money to fulfill your fondest dreams and desires. Having lived in poverty in his youth, he'd had to scrape and claw his way to attain the kind of deference he now possessed. He was certainly going to enjoy it to the fullest.

Inside, he took the elevator to the third floor where the offices of Conrad, Mitchell, Kent, and Schriver were located. Each time he walked down this hall, he experienced a pang of disappointment. He initially wanted to open an office in New York City instead of New Jersey. Since John Conrad had already established his business here and had offered him a partnership, Slade agreed to stay, feeling he owed it to his friend and mentor.

"But don't forget," he'd told John. "I will eventually open an office in New York. You know that is my ultimate goal."

"Yes, I know," John had answered. "And when that happens, you'll have my blessing."

So until then, Slade would have to endure the commercial look of this building with its interior that did nothing to enhance the classy decor of Conrad, Mitchell's offices the way a Manhattan skyscraper might.

Stepping through the door of the financial management firm was like entering a different world from the one without. The soft hues of mauve and gray invited clients to unwind, de-stress, drop their defenses. That put them right where Slade and his partners wanted them. It was a sales strategy that Slade himself had devised. In the past, he had found that people became uptight when it came to investing huge amounts of money. But being exposed to soft lighting, soothing music, plush, cozy furnishings, and easy-on-the-eye colors helped clients to relax enough so that the firm could more easily gain their trust and confidence. This enabled Slade and the others to utilize their financial advisory skills to the fullest. Though people walked through the door fully intending to increase their income-earning capacity through investments, they were squeamish about handing over so much of their hard-earned cash to some middleman they hardly even knew.

Slade understood this, but he knew how to get people exactly where he wanted them. He also knew that someday he'd have that office in New York.

He was still at his desk at least an hour after everyone else had gone. Maybe if he'd gotten to the office on time . . . *Nah!* Last night had been worth an extra hour or two at work.

He leaned back in the chair to dictate some letters into a cassette recorder. The phone rang, and since no one else was around to answer, he picked it up.

"Conrad, Mitchell, Kent, and Schriver. Slade Mitchell speaking."

"Hello, this is Mrs. Haloran," came a small, quivery voice.

"Yes, what can I do for you?"

"About three months ago, I gave one of your men some money to invest, but I haven't received a statement yet. Could you check on it for me?"

"Sure, Mrs. Haloran, but you may not have received it because the secretaries get a little backed up once in a while."

"I guess you're right. It's just that paying out so much money at once has got me on edge. It was my life's savings, and just about all I had."

"I understand. It's a natural reaction. Tell you what, I'll check on it for you right now. Can you hold for a moment?"

"Yes. Thank you so much."

Slade pressed the hold button, then punched in some codes on his computer. In the database, he typed in HALORAN and clicked on the "search" button. He read the screen: "NOT FOUND."

Thinking it possible someone forgot to enter the data, Slade went into the file room where hard copies of all the paperwork were kept. He thumbed through the "H" drawer. Not there.

An inkling began to niggle at the back of his mind, but he ignored it.

Going back to the phone, he hit the flashing button. "Mrs. Haloran, whom did you see when you came in?"

"Oh, I don't remember his name. My memory isn't what it used to be."

"Do you have the agreement that you both signed?"

"Yes, it's right here, but I can't understand the handwriting on the signature."

Slade rubbed his eyes with thumb and fingertips of his free hand. "What did he look like?"

"He was a nice-looking young man. I think he had blond hair. Or was it brown?"

This was going nowhere. There were several nice-looking young men at Conrad, Mitchell. "Look, Mrs. Haloran, I'm the only one here right now. I'm sure one of the secretaries could track this down better than I can. Give me your phone number and I'll have someone call you back."

He took down the number on a message pad and placed it on his own secretary's desk. Arlene was especially good at tracking down anything that was lost, and he was relatively sure she would get to the root of the matter.

There came that niggling again, but he dismissed it. He had other important, more delightful things to think about.

Slade felt he was at an age when a man might begin to consider settling down. He'd led a pretty exciting life so far, but he knew he didn't have to give up any of it.

He'd been seeing Melissa Kilpatrick pretty steadily for a while now. Melissa was everything a man could want in a lifelong companion: beautiful, intelligent, fun-loving, and she didn't begrudge him any of his wild passions—such as skydiving. Fussing about the dangers of it wasn't what she was about, nor was complaining that he spent more time with his skydiving cronies than he did with her. As long as he showed up when he promised, she was happy. Especially so if he presented her with some delectable little trinket, such as a nice piece of jewelry. The latter stuck in his craw somewhat, but he figured that everybody had his or her faults, and he was no different.

Yessir, he would certainly put more thought into popping the question to Melissa. A lot more.

The next morning while at the office, Slade placed a phone call to his mother in Florida. Since he had become considerably wealthy, he kept her set up in a condo in Orlando and paid all her bills. It was the least he could do to make up for all she went through for his sake years ago. From as far back as he could recall, his mother had given him one hundred percent of herself. She had been both his mother and the family's breadwinner.

At first, she had protested. "No child of mine will have to support me," she'd declared.

"I'm not a child anymore, Mom. I have more than enough to take care of both of us."

"Doesn't matter. That money is yours. You've earned it."

"So have you."

He stood firm in his decision until she finally gave in out of sheer exhaustion.

Needing advice on this gnawing impulse to settle down, he dialed his mother's number. In Slade's opinion, the best counsel to be had came straight from his mother's lips. She may have ruined her own life when she was young and naive enough to get involved with his married scoundrel of a father, but that experience had wizened Lois Mitchell to the ways of the world. Slade had always found her advice to be sound and reliable in the past. Now was no different.

After the usual over-expressed greetings from his mother, there was some small talk between the two, then Slade broached the subject that was foremost on his mind.

"Uh, Mom, I need to ask you something."

"Shoot, Slade. No need to be coy with me." It was just like his mother to dispense with amenities.

"I've been thinking lately. Now that I'm past thirty..."

"Just barely," Lois reminded him.

"Whatever. Anyway, I sort of think this might be a good time to get married and start a family."

"Do you have anyone in mind?"

"Yes, actually, I do. Her name is Melissa."

"What's she like?"

"She's intelligent and fun. A real beauty, too."

"Uh-huh. Do you love her?"

"Well, . . . I . . . Mom, what a question to ask!"

"What's so strange about that? That's the first question anyone would ask."

"Well, okay, I . . . I guess I love her."

"*Guess?* You *guess* you love her?"

"Yeah. I think so."

"Oh, Slade." She puffed out her breath, and Slade could imagine her sadly shaking her head. He was surprised by her outburst. "Slade Mitchell, you'd better make sure you're in love before you marry anyone! It just wouldn't be fair to you or to her." He had no time to reply before the rest of it was thrown at him. "And you'd better make sure that she loves you, too! You wouldn't be happy in a one-sided marriage, and I'd hate to see you being used. And another thing," she went on, "don't get married just because you're going on thirty-one. Age has nothing to do with it."

Slade smiled to himself. "Mom, I knew I could count on you to set me straight."

"That's what mothers are for, son."

Around one o'clock in the afternoon, Arlene poked her permed blonde head in the door to Slade's office.

"You know that client you asked me to check out?"

"Mrs. Haloran. Yes, what about her?"

"I can't find a thing on her. I've been searching practically all morning."

Slade leaned back in his chair, rubbed his jaw. "Hmmm." This was a little strange. "Did you ask any of the other women if they'd heard of her?" He waved her into the office as he spoke.

Arlene softly closed the door, then took a seat across from him. "Yes, but no one recognizes the name."

There was an elongated period of silence except for the thump-thump-thump of Slade's fingertips strumming the shiny surface of his desk. Finally, wrinkling his forehead, he leaned forward a little. "I'd have thought that if anyone could find it, Arlene, you could."

Her blue eyes widened at what she must have taken as beratement. "I'm sorry, Slade. I tried my best to . . ."

That's not what I meant," he interrupted, waving a dismissive hand. "I meant that if *you* couldn't find it, someone doesn't want it to be found."

Her eyes widened again, this time in shock. "What are you saying, Slade?"

Leaning forward still more, he drew his eyebrows together. "In plain words, I'm saying that someone in this firm could be committing fraud."

Arlene shook her head violently. "No! No, Slade. You've got to be wrong. No one here would ever do such a thing!"

"That's what I've always thought, and I hope you're right, Arlene. But you know what sticklers John and I are about everyone making sure they keep all records up to date." He stood and raked his fingers through his meticulously styled hair. "In any case, I'm going to do some further checking. In the meantime, I want you to call and see if you can pry more information out of Mrs. Haloran."

After Arlene left, Slade sank back down into the softness of his chair, sat back, and stared at the ceiling. A long sigh escaped his lips. He hoped he was very, very wrong. But he couldn't think of any other viable explanation for it. He knew that other firms had tried it and rarely got away with it. He didn't relish the thought of being part of such a scheme. Guilt by association.

But he just *had* to be wrong.

If he wasn't, it turned out that someone he thought he knew and trusted—well, he really didn't know that person at all.

CHAPTER THREE

THERE WAS TO BE A PARTY AT SLADE'S TONIGHT, AND STASI didn't want to go. He'd invited her yesterday, as if he'd acted on the spur of the moment.

She recalled every word of their conversation. He'd found her lugging a box of printer paper up to her apartment. As usual, and though he had been on his way out, he offered his help. The box was heavy, and she wasn't above accepting.

After opening the door, she directed him to place the paper by the computer. Setting the box down, he had asked, "What do you use all this paper for?"

"I print out a lot of reports."

"Reports? What kind of reports?"

"I run an information bureau and do reports for my clients."

She went into the kitchen, and Slade followed.

"What kind of information do you provide to your clients?" he asked, accepting a can of soda she pulled out of the fridge.

"Oh," she said, leaning against the refrigerator in contemplation, "things like background info for corporations interested in buying other companies. Sometimes a law firm will hire me to locate assets of an individual who has reneged on a judgment."

Seeming interested, he hiked himself into a sitting position on top of the kitchen counter and asked, "Do you like it?"

"Most of it, but not all."

He took a swig of soda, then asked, "What part of it don't you like?"

The very thought of it made her wrinkle her nose. "There are some clients who need info on somebody for the purpose of enforcing a court order. You know, 'deadbeat dads.'"

"What's so bad about that? You're helping someone, aren't you?"

"It's not that. It's the way I have to go about it. Sometimes deceit is involved to obtain the pertinent information."

"You mean you have to lie?"

"To put it bluntly, yes."

"But what's wrong with it if you're getting these guys to pay their child support?"

"You know I'm a born-again Christian and against any form of lying."

"Is that it? That's the big reason?"

Stasi had felt strangely uncomfortable and transparent at that moment, as distorted images of a coffin and an angry woman screaming accusations at her swept through her mind. She had despised any kind of lying since that incident. Being a Christian *wasn't* the only reason, but she couldn't tell him all of it.

"It's enough for me," she finally answered.

He hopped off the counter. "How do you handle those clients?"

"If I can't approach the case honestly, I refer it to a private investigator."

"I guess that ties it up neatly for you." Looking at his watch, he said, "I have to go, but . . . I'm having a party tomorrow night, and I'd like you to come."

He seemed hesitant, but so was she. "Uh, no, I don't think so."

"Why not? It'll be fun. Some of the other neighbors will be there, along with people from my office."

"Really, I'm not a party person . . ."

"I insist," he said, moving toward the door. "Eight sharp. Be there." He was gone before she could protest further.

Even now, as she prepared to go, she knew it would be a big mistake.

Standing before the closet, she decided that everyone would be sporting fancy threads, and she wanted to blend in. Opting for a classic look, she chose a simple black sleeveless sheath and added a single strand of pearls for contrast. Quickly running a brush through her dense black mane, she left her hair loose and flowing around her shoulders. After slipping into a pair of soft, black leather pumps, she was ready.

Stepping into the corridor, she could hear loud music wafting from Slade's apartment. Murmurs and bursts of laughter told her she was already late. Or *fashionably* late, as she preferred to think of it.

Stasi rang the bell and waited. No answer. She tried the doorknob, and it turned, so she stepped in.

Inside, she was immediately accosted by blaring rock music, the beat of which reverberated through every bone and nerve in her body. Alcohol was flowing freely, and here and there, couples could be seen locked in passionate embraces.

Slade approached her. "Hello, Stasi. Glad you could make it. Help yourself to food and drinks." He indicated a table set up against the far wall laden with an inviting array of food and beverages.

"Thanks, Slade, I'll do that." She walked toward the table with the uncomfortable feeling that his eyes were boring into her back.

Slade watched her glide away from him, thinking how great she looked tonight. Even though she dressed simply, she outshone most of the women in the room. Their faces were caked with make-up, and their dresses—well, the women were practically falling out of them. He imagined they thought this glamorous and appealing, much the same as Melissa did. He sighed and swung his eyes toward the woman he had been contemplating growing old with, then moved his gaze back to Stasi. She wore little make-up and still managed to look glamorous but in a classy way. Not only did she dress with class, but also her facial features were unique. It wasn't so much her sapphire blue eyes that caught his attention but that jawline. It was squared off, in no way detracting from her beauty but only *enhancing* it.

After mingling with some of the neighbors, Stasi sat off in a corner alone with a plate of finger foods. This was the first time she'd been in Slade's apartment, so she took the opportunity to admire the decor. She thought it suited him perfectly. All modern and geometric, black-and-white, leather, chrome, and glass, set off by a plush gray carpet.

She was regarding the artwork on the walls when her gaze locked on to a tall, lean, blond man wearing a green Henley with khaki pants. Carrying a drink, he floated from woman to woman, whispering in an ear, circling an arm intimately around a shoulder, placing a peck on the lips. He was handsome, and he knew it. A lot like Slade.

Averting her eyes long enough to select a tidbit from her plate to nibble on, she was taken aback when she lifted her eyes to find the object of her scrutiny standing before her. There was no way to avoid him.

"Hello, pretty lady," he said in a silky voice.

She nodded slightly, then bit into a cube of cheese, hoping it would deflect his attention.

"Is this seat taken?" he asked, pointing to a chair next to hers.

"Uh . . . no, but . . ."

"Good, then you won't mind if I sit here." He sat down and offered his hand. "The name's Troy Kent."

Stasi reluctantly shook his fingertips. "Anastasia Courtland."

"Would you like a drink?"

"Yes, thank you. Ginger ale." Maybe he wouldn't come back.

"That's it? Just ginger ale?"

"That's it."

"Okay." He stood up, lifted a lock of her hair, and gave it a soft tug. "You got it," he said, then moved swiftly toward the table.

Slade slid into the seat that Troy had just vacated. "He's not your type, Stasi."

She glanced at him. "How would you know?"

"Because I know him well. He's one of my business partners. He's a womanizer. Can't commit. Never faithful. You'd do well to keep away from him."

"Don't worry, I've been watching him work the room. I know what to expect, and I can take care of myself."

"It's not that, it's just . . ."

"Believe me, I'll be fine."

Troy returned and handed Stasi a glass. "Here you are, hon." He sat in the chair on Stasi's other side and slid his arm around her shoulder. He began to lightly trail his fingertips up and down her arm.

In a low voice, Slade said, "Hey, Troy, why don't you back off. Give her some breathing space."

Before Troy could respond, Stasi said, "Slade, really, I'm fine. I'm a big girl and can take care of myself."

"But I don't think . . ."

"Go ahead, Slade, take the lady's advice. She's safe with me."

He opened his mouth to say something, but Stasi silenced him with a glare.

"Okay, you win," he said, raising his hands in surrender. "I hope you know what you're doing." He stood and walked over to where Melissa had taken in the whole scene. Stasi watched as Slade try to assuage her, but anger flared in the young woman's green eyes as she tossed a stray lock of honey blonde hair over her shoulder with an impatient flick of her hand.

"That's better," Troy said with a smirk that made Stasi want to strip it off his face like so much packing tape.

"Oh, I wouldn't say that."

"Are you toying with me, little lady?"

"Oh, no, I never toy with people."

He leaned closer, pulling her tighter, and whispered, "I don't think I'd mind if you did."

She let out a short laugh. "That's not saying much for yourself."

He gazed deeply into her eyes. "It's just that when I stare into those gorgeous blue eyes of yours, I turn to putty."

She rolled her eyes and shook her head, as she placed her plate on the empty chair beside her. *Oh, brother!*

Troy fanned himself with his hand. "It's getting awful hot in here with all these people. Why don't we go to your place, where I'm sure it's much cooler?"

Give me a break!

"I have a better idea," she said, flicking an imaginary piece of lint from his shoulder. "It will cool you off, and you won't even have to leave that chair." Before he caught on, she hooked a finger in his collar and poured her ginger ale down his shirt.

Troy gasped and jumped up. "What'd you do that for?"

Stasi looked up at him in feigned, wide-eyed innocence. "You said you were warm."

He growled and stalked off toward the bathroom amid peals of laughter and a round of applause.

Stasi went over to Slade. With an air of arrogance, he stood braced against the wall. His legs formed the number four, while the toe of his shoe rested on the carpet. "Thank you for inviting me, but I'm leaving now."

"So soon? If it's Troy you're worried about, I'll make sure he doesn't bother you again."

She shook her head. "No, it's not that. I just . . . I don't belong here."

He nodded as if he fully understood what she meant. "Okay. By the way, nice performance."

She flashed him a smile, then turned and headed for the door.

As he watched her leave, Slade thought: *Well, well, what do you know? The lady really* can *take care of herself.*

He had been attracted to Stasi right from the beginning, but knowing she was a Christian had dimmed that attraction. As a result, he had tried to keep his distance, avoiding her whenever possible. But he'd eventually encounter her from time to time with no avenue of escape. Then his desire to be in her company would become so strong—as it had the other day when he had invited her to the party—that he'd find himself doing anything to be around her.

Still, he just wanted to remain on friendly terms with her. Knowing about her faith made him feel protective of her, especially around the type of people with whom he associated. He should never have insisted on her coming. It made him feel that exposing her to his lifestyle could somehow mar her purity.

It was ridiculous to think this way, he knew.

Anyhow, after tonight, he could see that she didn't need his protection after all.

CHAPTER FOUR

THE FIRST THING MONDAY MORNING, SLADE WENT STRAIGHT TO John Conrad's office. John and Slade were the first to start the firm eight years ago. Slade was green then, but John was some years older, with plenty of experience, and he taught Slade everything he knew. Of course, Slade had developed some of his own techniques over the years, but he trusted and admired John, remaining great friends with him.

He knocked on the door of John's office, then entered without waiting for an answer.

John looked up from his cluttered desk. He wasn't as orderly as Slade, except in his style of dress. Always impeccable.

"Hey, Slade. I'm surprised to see you out and about. You're usually still in bed recovering from the weekend this early on a Monday morning."

Had he detected a slight tone of hostility in John's voice? Slade was apparently mistaken in his assumption that no one minded his occasional tardiness.

"Morning, John. I came in early because I wanted to talk to you about something before the others arrived."

"Sure, have a seat."

Slade sat in a burgundy leather chair across the desk from John. "This is a pretty delicate matter, John."

"I'm listening," he said, nodding once.

"One night last week, I was here alone when a woman called about her account. I tried looking her name up in the database, but it wasn't there."

"Someone probably forgot to enter the information. That happens sometimes."

"That's what I thought at first. But the next day, I had Arlene do an all-out search for hard copies of the papers the woman had signed. You know Arlene is the best when it comes to finding lost files and papers, but she came up empty."

John leaned forward, raising his eyebrows. His wire frame glasses slid down his nose a fraction of an inch. "Slade, what are you saying?"

"I guess I'm saying that I think something funny is going on. I wanted to come to you first. I'm not sure what to do about it."

John jumped out of his chair, and his outburst startled Slade. "I can't believe this! You're accusing someone in this firm of illegal dealings? How could you?"

"Take it easy, John. I'm not accusing anyone. I'm hoping there's some logical explanation for it. I just wanted you to know, that's all."

John took a deep breath and relaxed back into his chair. "I'm sorry, Slade. Of course, you did the right thing in coming to me.

Why don't you forget it, and I'll look into it. There probably is an explanation for it."

Slade stood up. "Sure, John. And I'm sorry if I insulted you. I realize that in essence, I'm questioning the integrity of this firm. And you and I . . . well, we *are* the firm."

"No need to apologize, Slade. It's just that you took me by surprise with this. It's a little hard to swallow."

"I understand. Let me know what you find out." Slade left John's office and headed for his own.

Back at his desk, Slade couldn't concentrate on work. He threw the pen he'd been using down on the desk and rubbed his eyes. Maybe he shouldn't have put this whole thing on John's shoulders. He'd feel better if he came up with some solid evidence, then he and John could do something about it together.

He'd made up his mind. Tonight, when everyone else was gone, he would do a little investigating on his own.

It was seven o'clock when the last workers left the office. Slade waited five more minutes, then turned to his computer terminal. He didn't want anyone walking in on him while he did this.

He thought that since Mrs. Haloran's name wasn't in the database, it might be in another file. Pulling up the computer directory, he scanned it for other file names. He found several that he wasn't familiar with, and he checked them out. Mrs. Haloran was not in any of them.

Toward the bottom of the list, Slade spotted a strange file named "rdtcomm." He opened the file to find an endless list of accounts, among which was Mrs. Haloran's.

This all seemed very strange to him. It was not the system the firm normally used for listing its clients. All clients were listed in the main database with all account information, then cross-referenced with the names of the companies they are invested with.

Continuing to search the file, he came across templates for various forms, letters, and statements, all headed with the company name of "RDT Communications, Inc."

Stranger still.

For one thing, he had never heard of this company. Secondly, the companies that Conrad, Mitchell dealt with all sent out their own statements and any other form of contact with the clients. Conrad, Mitchell only set up the initial portfolio but received copies of any mail sent to the clients.

Why were there forms in this file? There could be only one answer, and the thought of what it was made the blood drain from his head down to his toes.

Slade decided to make a copy of the complete file to take home for further review. While waiting for the computer to complete the task, he impulsively dialed John's home number, figuring he'd arrived home by now.

When John answered his phone, Slade said, "John, I won't keep you long."

"No problem, Slade. What is it?"

"Remember what we discussed in your office today?"

"Remember? It's been the only thing on my mind since."

"Well, in relation to that, check out a file on the computer named 'rdtcomm' when you have a free minute."

Slade heard John clear his throat. "Uh, sure, I'll get on it as soon as possible."

"Good. I think it will explain a lot of things."

"Of course. Have you read the entire file?"

"Not yet, but I'm making a copy to take home for further scrutiny."

"Good thinking. Get back to me after you've done that, and we'll compare notes."

"Will do, John. Gotta run!"

After hanging up the phone, Slade removed the floppy from the disk drive and dropped it into the inner pocket of his suit jacket. He would find a safe place to keep it at home.

CHAPTER FIVE

THE PHONE ON THE TABLE BESIDE HIM RANG, AND THE MAN picked it up. "Hello?"

"It's me."

"Yeah. What's up?"

"It appears that we've run into a little snag in our operation."

"What do you mean?"

"Mitchell is becoming suspicious."

"But how?"

"Rumor has it that one of our 'special' clients called while he was alone at the office and there was no info in the computer."

"We always knew there was a possibility that that could happen, but we figured that we'd be able to cover it up easily enough. What went wrong?"

"Mitchell went wrong. He's smart. Not to mention that he's excruciatingly honest when it comes to his business. He couldn't stand seeing his precious firm's name being dragged through the mud. I hear he found the file for a bogus company in the directory and made a copy to take home. I don't have to tell you what he'll do with it once he figures out what it's for."

"So what do we do?"

"You have an outing coming up on Saturday, don't you?"

"Yes."

"I'd like you to take care of the situation."

"How do you mean?"

"Do I have to spell it out for you?"

His blood turned to ice. "N-no! You can't mean it!"

"I do."

"But do we have to go *that* far?"

"If we don't, the situation will only worsen. Mitchell will never give up until he knows everything."

"I don't know. Can't you do it?"

"No. And I'm sure when you think about it, you'll understand why."

"I still don't know. Conning people is one thing, but this is something else altogether."

"Listen, I don't like the idea any better than you do, but what's better? To nip this thing in the bud or spend half your life in prison?"

"Okay, I get your point. You sure do know what buttons to push."

"Yeah. If I didn't, I wouldn't be where I am today."

His hand shook as he hung up the phone. His whole body was shaking. He didn't want to do this and never should have gotten himself involved in the first place.

Sitting on the sofa, he wrung his hands, then raked them through his hair. He'd come this far, and there was no turning back.

Actually, it wasn't such a difficult decision to make. He'd simply choose the lesser of the two evils. After all, it far surpassed the idea of a long-term prison sentence.

CHAPTER SIX

ON SATURDAY MORNING, STASI WAS TAKING OUT THE GARBAGE and ran into Slade at the elevator. It was evident by the large, green plastic bag he toted that he had the same destination in mind. Not having seen much of him since the party, she suddenly felt awkward around him and couldn't fathom why.

He reached for her bag. "Here, let me take that for you."

"Oh, no, thank you. I can handle it." She averted her eyes.

"I know you can handle it. I'm just trying to be gentlemanly."

"I know that. You always are, but really, I can handle it."

Exasperated, he yanked the bag from her grasp. "I know you can handle it. I found out just how tough you are at the party the other night. But can't you at least give me the satisfaction of exercising my masculine abilities?"

She laughed, and just then the elevator doors slid open. "I've no doubt you've plenty of opportunity to do *that*."

Pressing a forearm against the frame to keep the doors from closing, he frowned at her.

"Well," she sighed, "I really have no reason to go down now, do I?"

"Sure, you do."

"Oh? And what might that be?"

"I need some company." He smiled mischievously.

She winced inwardly. *So cocksure of himself.* "Oh, all right," she acquiesced, without knowing why, and stepped onto the elevator. Glancing at his attire, she noticed he wore a peculiar sort of jumpsuit. "Where are you headed?" she asked. "After the dumpster, I mean."

"Skydiving." His eyes glittered.

"Really? It sounds exciting!"

"It is. It's my passion! You've never tried it?"

The elevator bumped to a stop, and the doors swished open.

"No."

"I think you'd like it," Slade said.

"I'm not sure. Maybe someday I'll get up enough nerve to try it." She watched him toss the bags into the dumpster. They weren't heavy by any means, but he made them seem as light as Wiffle balls.

"Let me know when you're ready. I'll coach you, even go with you," he told her as they reentered the building.

"Wouldn't Melissa have something to say about that?"

"Probably." He leaned close to her. "But I never pass up an opportunity to spend time with a beautiful woman."

Still so cocky. Would he ever change?

They were silent on the ride back up to their floor. When the elevator came to a stop and they stepped out, Stasi said, "Enjoy your . . . adventure."

"You know I will," he said, grinning, then disappeared into his apartment.

Stasi remained in the hall. Leaning against her door, she sighed, shook her head and thought, *If only* . . .

What Stasi didn't know was that Slade was standing just inside his own door thinking the exact same thing.

Putting an end to his preposterous thoughts, Slade pushed himself away from where he had been leaning against the door and walked over to the end table, where he had left the cordless phone. After punching in the numbers, he glanced at his watch. Nine twenty-five. Just enough time.

The phone rang twice before being picked up.

"Hello?"

"John. Slade here."

"Yes, Slade?"

"I'm leaving in about four minutes, but I just wanted to tell you that I had a chance to study that disk last night, and I found some pretty incriminating stuff."

"You what?"

"Look, I'm in a hurry, but I think the two of us should look it over together so we can decide what to do. Gotta go! See ya!"

"Slade, wait!"

As he removed the phone from his ear, he could hear John's plea. He had no time to get into it now, so he hung up.

At precisely nine-thirty, Slade's doorbell rang. He knew it would be Troy Kent picking him up to go skydiving.

Slade and Troy had become increasingly friendly over the past year. Slade discovered that Troy was much like him: a bold, go-getting risk taker and an adventurous, fun-loving womanizer, the latter of which he wasn't so sure he should be proud of. They had many of the same interests, skydiving being one of them. Every two weeks, Slade and Troy got together with a couple of other men from the firm for the thrill of the free-fall.

Slade opened the door. "Hey, Troy. Just let me gather up my gear and I'm all ready."

"Sure, pal."

Slade reached for his skydiving gear, which he'd earlier placed against the wall by the door. "Let's go!"

Down at the car, Troy told Slade to go ahead and get in. Taking Slade's gear from him, he said, "I'll be a minute or so. I'll have to rearrange some things in the trunk to fit this in."

Slade slid into the passenger seat and waited, but Troy hadn't taken too long. In no time he was behind the wheel, and they were on their way to a drop zone in Williamstown, about a thirty-five-minute ride from Haddonfield.

The others, Clark Schriver, a partner in the firm, and Darrell Boyd, an associate, were waiting and ready to roll when they arrived at the small airport.

"We have to hurry. The rest of the load's already on the plane, and they're getting impatient," Clark said.

Slade was glad he'd done a gear check at home when he'd carefully packed it. There wouldn't have been time for it now.

"Let me get your chute and help you with it," Clark offered.

"Okay."

Clark readied Slade's chute while Darrell helped Troy. After Slade slipped on his goggles and fastened his altimeter, Clark handed him the chute and strapped it on. "Let's rock!" he said, giving Clark the thumbs-up.

The four of them ran out to the plane, where other men and women were waiting to go up. They had barely jumped on before the plane took off down the short runway. Minutes later they were airborne.

The small plane circled the airport, gaining altitude. The pilot had previously been advised that this load wanted to jump at fourteen thousand feet, so he kept the plane at a steady climb.

Slade sat on the bench in anticipation of the thrill to come. He loved doing this! It gave him a feeling of freedom that he never experienced in any other way.

"Slade," Darrell yelled over the clamorous hum of the plane's motor. "Part of your pilot chute's sticking out of the pack. Want me to stuff it back in?"

"Uh . . . Yeah, sure, Darrell," Slade yelled back. "Thanks." He thought he'd been careful when he packed his gear, but he was surprised by Darrell's concern. Darrell normally wouldn't have cared if Slade's whole chute was hanging out.

There was some tension between Slade and Darrell at the office. Darrell sorely wanted to be made partner in the firm, but Slade felt he wasn't ready and hadn't agreed when he and the other partners met to discuss it. Somehow, Darrell found out about it and confronted Slade. Slade stood his ground, and Darrell hadn't been very congenial toward him since.

Darrell seemed to be taking longer than necessary to fix the chute. "Is it okay, now, Darrell?" he asked, slanting a peek over his shoulder.

"Yeah, almost got it." He gave the pack a pat. "There you go." He smiled at Slade, and the flash of his white teeth contrasted with his ebony skin.

Reaching the desired altitude, the pilot gave the signal, and one by one, the jumpers filed out, whooping and hollering like cowboys.

Assuming the free-fall position—belly down, knees bent, arms spread and curved at the elbow—Slade experienced the familiar tingle ripple through his body that always occurred within the first few seconds of the jump.

As always, the panoramic view below was breathtaking. The others gracefully descended nearby, as if participants in some ethereal fairy dance.

Slade checked his altimeter. A couple of hundred more feet and he'd open his chute.

The speed of the free-fall is so great that the distance was covered almost immediately. Slade reached back for the throw-out ball located in a small pouch on the back of his pack. The other jumpers were doing the same.

To Slade's horror, the cord that normally attaches the ball to the pilot chute was severed. He reached for the cutaway handle that would allow him to rid himself of the main canopy and use the reserve chute. This time, he was doubly horrified. The cord on the cutaway handle was also severed, which meant that the main canopy would hinder deployment of the reserve chute.

He ripped open the flap to the compartment on the straps that crisscrossed his chest and pulled the reserve pin. The reserve chute began to open, but because the main canopy was still attached, there was only partial deployment as the chutes became entangled.

Malfunction of both chutes resulted in a tumble of Slade's body, pitching him headlong and tangling his feet in the lines.

It all happened in a matter of seconds, but now Slade was falling fast, and the shouts from the others faded into nothingness as their open chutes slowed their progression. All he could hear now was the wind thundering in his ears as he plunged toward the earth at breakneck speed.

Daring to look down at the kaleidoscope of green, brown, and yellow spiraling toward him, Slade saw that he was headed for a clump of trees. At that moment, he realized he would either die or be very seriously injured.

In seconds, he found himself bumped and jostled about while plunging through a jungle of leaves and branches that clawed his face and limbs as he dropped heavily through.

He was knocked out, and never knew that he hit the ground.

CHAPTER SEVEN

HE WATCHED AS THE EMERGENCY CREW WORKED TO REMOVE Slade from the tree. Hanging upside down a mere two feet from the ground, Slade's feet were tangled in the line of the chute, which was caught in the tree.

They said he was still alive.

He'd blundered and would probably never live it down. How was he supposed to fix it? Slade would undoubtedly be in a hospital for some time to come. He couldn't just walk in there and shoot him. *Hi, pal, how ya feelin'? Pow! Pow! Pow!*

Ridiculous.

He'd have to think of something—and fast—before Slade realized there was a connection to this "accident" and what he'd stumbled upon at the office.

CHAPTER EIGHT

ON TUESDAY AFTERNOON, AFTER A MEETING WITH ONE OF her clients, Stasi emerged from her car and passed Slade's Jaguar on her way to the building. She hadn't seen him in the past few days, nor had she noticed any activity around his apartment.

Letting herself into her own apartment, she dropped her purse and keys on the small table by the entrance and made her way into the kitchen. Taking a plastic container of beef stew from the refrigerator, she placed it in the microwave. While she waited, she took out a roll and butter and set it on the dining table.

Maybe she should ring Slade's doorbell. He could be sick or something, and perhaps she could help him out. Leaving the roll and butter on the table, she left the apartment.

Outside Slade's apartment, Stasi pushed the button to the left of the door and listened to the chime from within. After a minute, she rang again. When there was still no answer, she knew he probably wasn't there and left.

Back in her apartment, she scooped the stew into a bowl, opened a can of soda, then sat down to eat.

Buttering her bread, she wondered why Slade wasn't home, yet his car was parked outside. Of course, someone else could have driven him to work, but that didn't seem likely. Slade loved driving that car, she knew. But the Jag had sat there all weekend, and she hadn't seen or heard from Slade since Saturday.

Finished with her meal, she carried the bowl over to the sink and ran water into it, then tossed the soda can into the recycling bin.

Perhaps she should call his office. But what would she say? *Oh, hi, just checking up on you.* He'd think she was a nut. Yet, she had the strangest feeling that something was not right.

Flipping through the phone book, she wondered why she should have this strong urge to make sure Slade was all right. When she found his office number, she picked up the phone from the end table beside the sofa and punched in the number.

"Conrad, Mitchell, Kent, and Schriver. How may I help you?" came a musical female voice.

"Hello, my name is Stasi Courtland. I'm a neighbor of Slade Mitchell. Would he happen to be there?"

"Oh. Uh . . . you haven't heard?"

Her heart rate went up a notch. "Heard what?"

"Mr. Mitchell has been in a terrible accident."

Stasi's throat went dry. "What kind of accident? Is he all right?"

"It was a skydiving accident on Saturday. He's in a coma at Kennedy Memorial in Washington Township."

"Thank you." Stasi hung up before the other woman had a chance to say more and was instantly out the door.

Twenty-five minutes later, Stasi pulled into the parking lot of Kennedy Memorial Hospital. Once inside, she approached the desk and asked for Slade's room number. The woman informed her he was in intensive care on the second floor and only immediate family members were allowed to visit. Admitting that she wasn't related to Slade, Stasi asked if she could at least go to that floor and obtain information on Slade's condition from the nurses. The receptionist said she could.

On the second floor, Stasi headed for the nurse's station. A short, middle-aged woman with red hair teased into a bubble looked up at her inquiringly.

"Hello. Would I be able to speak with anyone about Slade Mitchell's condition?"

"Are you family?"

"No, but I'm a close neighbor."

"Then I can't give you any information." The woman must have taken pity on Stasi when she saw her face fall, because she added, "You could wait for the doctor to make his rounds. It would be up to him if he wanted to tell you anything."

"Sure, when will he be in?"

"Not for a while, I'm afraid. It could be anywhere from an hour to five hours."

"Thanks. I'll stay for a little while. Is there a waiting area nearby?"

The nurse pointed with her pen. "There's a small waiting room down the hall to the left."

"Thanks, again."

The little waiting room was furnished with several chairs and a television. Stasi sat down and dug into her purse for her cell phone to make sure it was turned on should she receive a business call, but noticing a sign prohibiting them, she turned it off.

She looked around. The only other person there was an older woman who sat gazing dazedly up at the screen of the TV, which sat on a shelf bolted high up on a wall. She wondered if this woman could be here for Slade. His mother, perhaps? No one she recognized as any of Slade's friends showed up the entire time she waited.

Two hours later, Stasi was ready to retch from the combination of antiseptic and sickroom odors typical of a hospital. As she contemplated getting some fresh air, a young doctor approached her. His blond hair was short but thick, and when he smiled at her, his blue eyes sparkled.

"Hello. I'm Dr. Blanchard, Slade Mitchell's doctor. Are you the young woman waiting to speak with me?"

Stasi stood up and extended her hand. "Yes, my name is Stasi Courtland. I realize that I can't see him just yet but can you tell me anything about his condition? I've heard he's in a coma."

"You're not a relative?"

"No."

He looked thoughtful. "Well, I can tell you that he *is* in a coma with serious head injuries sustained in his fall."

Her next question was one she wasn't sure she wanted to hear the answer to, but she asked it anyway. "Will he . . . make it?"

The doctor sighed. "There are never any guarantees with an injury of this type, but his chances are good." Then he dropped the bomb. "Of course, once he comes out of it, he'll probably have some serious problems to deal with."

"Such as . . .?"

"Probably some form of paralysis or extremity weakness. But we won't know for sure until he's awake. Though we must be thankful that he landed in a tree. Otherwise, he wouldn't even be alive."

Stasi felt lightheaded and sat down. Looking up at the doctor, she asked, "Have many people been in to visit him? I'm not sure if he has any family nearby."

"On the first day there was a group of about eight people in the waiting area. But then, in the past two days, he's had only a few here and there. Though there is another young woman who is here regularly in the evenings."

"Oh, that must be his girlfriend, Melissa."

"I believe so. I've had the staff try to determine whether there is any family we should notify. This Melissa said he mentioned a mother in another state, but she had never met her, nor can she recall which state."

"I'll ask around our apartment complex, and if I find out anything, I'll let the hospital know."

"We'd certainly appreciate it."

"I'm just going to wait around awhile in case he comes out of it."

"You may be waiting for a long time. It could be weeks, even months before he wakes up."

"I understand. I'll just come by as much as I can."

The doctor hesitated before leaving and silently regarded for a moment. "Miss Courtland, I'll tell you what. Since no one's been here today, why don't I take you in to see him for just a minute? It may do him good to sense someone's presence. Someone who cares about him the way you seem to."

"You're sure it's all right?"

He grinned. "Doctor's orders."

Pulling herself up straight and stiff, she replied, "Must obey doctor's orders." Then her face softened as she said, "Thank you, Dr. Blanchard."

"You're welcome." He then took her by the arm and guided her through the doors to ICU.

At the first sight of Slade, shock waves rippled through her body. He was unrecognizable. His face, bruised and swollen, was also dotted with various cuts. Bloodstained bandages covered his head. He lay motionless, attached to a tangle of tubes, and a machine made a constant blipping sound. This did not seem at all the man who she knew possessed so much vitality and zest for life.

Reaching for his hand, she stopped and looked at the doctor, who nodded his approval.

Slade's hand was lifeless.

Seeing him like this, she felt a strong urge to pray sweep over her. She dropped to her knees at the bedside and whispered all that lay on her heart to the only One she knew could help Slade now.

When she finished, it was time to leave, but she intended to come back as often as she could.

CHAPTER NINE

STASI SAT BY THE HOSPITAL BED WAITING FOR SOME SIGN of life. It had been a week since the accident, and Slade was still out. The doctor told her that it was likely that the longer he was out, the greater the chance of brain damage. She didn't want to think about that, and she knew that Slade would be devastated by the prospect. It was incomprehensible to think that a man of such intelligence, who exuded so much charm and vitality could . . .

Stop it! She wouldn't let herself think it.

Every moment she could spare, which amounted to at least once every day, was spent at the hospital. Sometimes she visited twice—day and evening. The knowledge that the number of visitors had tapered off after only one week left her heart aching for Slade. But she didn't understand why she should be so concerned.

Instead of dwelling on the unexplained, she just kept up her ritual. She would sit for hours, holding his hand, talking incessantly about anything and everything, just so he would know someone was there. At least, she hoped he knew. Then, when she became hoarse from the constant monologue, she would kneel by his bed in whispered prayer.

The only other person Stasi encountered during her visits was Melissa. At first, she was always there on the same evenings as Stasi. Then, the visits gradually became less frequent. But whenever Melissa did come, she barely spoke—with her mouth, anyway. Her eyes and body language did all the talking. They practically shouted her resentment at Stasi's presence.

Stasi rose from the chair and pushed it aside. Dropping by the bedside, she silently implored God to help Slade. Praying was as vital to her as breathing, but now, she wondered why the burden of it lay so heavily on her heart. Perhaps it was Slade's only hope.

CHAPTER TEN

HER FINGERS FLEW OVER THE COMPUTER KEYBOARD. BECAUSE she had been spending so much time at the hospital, Stasi had gotten a little behind in her work.

Another week had gone by, and Slade still had not come around. Consequently, she found it hard to concentrate on her work. Sighing heavily, she turned off the computer and moved toward the kitchen to pour herself a cup of coffee. The cordless phone she had left lying on the counter jangled loudly, causing her to jump and spill a few drops of coffee as she poured.

Immediately putting down the coffee pot and cup, she dashed for the phone, hoping it was the hospital with good news. Because she visited so often, the nurses had come to know her, and she had given them her phone number should Slade awaken.

"Hello?" she said breathlessly.

"Hello, is this Stasi Courtland?"

"Yes. Yes, it is."

"I'm calling from Kennedy Memorial. You asked us to call if there were any changes concerning Mr. Mitchell."

"Yes. What kind of change has there been?" Her heart began pounding.

"He's come out of the coma. . ."

"I'll be right there!" Plunking down the phone, she hoped that the woman understood that she was too excited to listen to any more and that she wanted to get there as soon as possible.

Stasi arrived at the hospital fifteen minutes later. She walked into the room that Slade had been transferred to the week before and saw that not only was the doctor there but also Melissa was present.

"Ah, Miss Courtland. We were just talking about you," Dr. Blanchard remarked.

"You were?" she asked, as she walked toward Slade's bed. "I hope you were saying good things about me."

"As a matter of fact, I was. I've been telling Slade how you've kept vigil by his side for many hours through this ordeal."

She colored slightly as she felt Melissa's eyes burning into her. She didn't know what the woman had against her. There was never any indication of more than friendship between Slade and her. But she supposed that if the shoe were on the other foot, she'd also be suspicious of another female hanging around.

Having avoided it long enough, she finally looked down at Slade. The cuts and bruises were almost gone now, leaving a light yellowish-purple hue.

"I know this is a silly question, but how are you feeling?"

"L-like I . . . was . . . run o-ver b-by a t-truck." He spoke slowly and with a slight slur.

She gave him a sad smile.

"I d-don't . . . re-member how . . . I got . . . h-here."

Stasi flashed a worried look at Melissa and Dr. Blanchard, the latter giving her a knowing glance. She patted Slade's arm for reassurance. "Don't worry, I'm sure it will all come back to you."

"Slade," Dr. Blanchard began. "You've had a terrible accident."

Slade looked at him in puzzlement. "Ac-cident? What k-kind?"

"Skydiving. Apparently, your parachute malfunctioned."

"Skydiving?" Slade looked incredulous. "But . . .but th-that's ridic-ulous!" he sputtered.

"Nevertheless, that's how it happened, Slade. Now, I think you should get some sleep. This has all been very strenuous for you." To the two women, he said, "Why don't we talk out in the hall?" He motioned for them to precede him out the door.

"J-just . . . woke up," Slade protested.

"I know, but right now, rest is the best thing for you."

Melissa kissed Slade. "Bye, honey. I'll be back soon."

Slade looked down and noticed that Melissa had hold of his left hand. His face registered confusion, then horror. He looked at Melissa, terror in his eyes. "I c-can't . . . feel you h-holding my . . . h-hand!"

Melissa appeared stricken, not knowing what to say to Slade. Looking at the doctor, her eyes clearly conveyed her helplessness.

Dr. Blanchard immediately walked over to Slade. "We'll talk later, Slade. Right now, you need to rest. Don't excite yourself. I'll send a nurse in with something to help you sleep." With that, he ushered the two women through the door, closing it against Slade's objections.

In the hall, Stasi and Melissa followed the doctor to the nurse's station and waited while he gave orders. Then Dr. Blanchard turned to the women.

"I've examined Slade. It appears his head trauma resulted in what we call a mixed deficit."

"What exactly is a mixed deficit?" Melissa asked.

"It's a sort of paralysis that is more dominant on one side of the body, less severe on the other. In Slade's case, his left is more severely affected than his right."

Melissa slouched and hid her face in her hands. Stasi felt for her and placed a reassuring arm around her shoulder.

Since Melissa appeared incapacitated, at the moment, Stasi addressed the doctor with a question she knew Melissa would want an answer to. "Will he ever be the same?"

The doctor stared gravely at the floor. "Probably not. Slade was in excellent physical shape before the accident. He will probably regain some of his ability, but I'm afraid that he'll be left with some degree of a permanent disability.

"No!" Melissa tore free of Stasi's arm and ran down the hall, screaming her denial all the way.

"Melissa wait!" Stasi wanted to run after her but stopped herself. It was probably better to let her be alone for now.

Sighing heavily, she turned back to the doctor. "Thank you."

Dr. Blanchard nodded and, placing a hand on her shoulder, gave it a slight squeeze.

Stasi turned and floated down the corridor as if in a fog. She barely realized that the excessive pounding she heard in her ears was coming from her own heart.

Passing Slade's room again, she peeked in and saw that he was sleeping soundly from whatever the doctor had ordered the nurse to give him. She hoped he had been out before Melissa ran screaming down the hall.

How will he react when he's told that he'll never be the same again?

CHAPTER ELEVEN

THE TWO MEN SELECTED A CORNER TABLE IN THE DIMLY LIT seclusion of a seldom patronized tavern and ordered drinks.

"I guess our little problem has solved itself," one said after the waitress left.

"How so?" the other asked.

"He didn't die, but he can't remember anything."

"I still can't see how that solves the problem."

He stared at the other man as if he were dense. "If he can't remember anything, that means we're safe."

The other man reached over and roughly cuffed him on the shoulder. "Dimwit! Did you ever stop to think that his memory might return?"

"Yeah," he said while rubbing his shoulder. "Briefly. But I figured we were safe for the time being, and *if* he recovers his memory, we could take care of the situation then."

"We can't wait until then," the other man said, his voice tight. "Suppose we don't get to him before he gets to the authorities?"

The waitress appeared with their drinks and deposited them on the table, then sashayed away.

"This is true." He lowered his voice and continued. "But as I said in the beginning, I don't really relish the idea of murder. I never thought it would come this far."

"Neither did I, but it has, and now we have to do what we have to do. More important, we have to find that disk. If it gets into the wrong hands, we're done."

"This is also true," the other man said, raising his glass in a salute. "Looks like now we have *two* big jobs on our hands," he said before throwing back his scotch.

CHAPTER TWELVE

"I CAN'T GET OVER IT, RACHEL. I MEAN, THE GUY LOOKS SO helpless lying in that hospital bed. He's nothing like he used to be."

Stasi sat across from her friend Rachel Darrow in the small restaurant where they occasionally had lunch together after church on Sundays. She had been expressing her anxiety over Slade's condition for the past fifteen minutes.

"Relax, Stasi. Why are you so upset about this?"

"Slade is a neighbor of mine, but I would hate to see *anyone* in his situation. Wouldn't you feel the same?"

"I would, but . . ." Rachel cocked her dark, curly-haired head to one side and raised a well-shaped eyebrow at Stasi. "You're a little more upset than I would be if it happened to a casual neighbor of mine. I would say *distressed* is a better word to describe it."

Stasi ignored this and pretended to be interested in forking up her lunch.

"Didn't you tell me that this guy was sort of wild and that you disliked hanging out with him and his crowd?"

After swallowing the mouthful of salad she'd been chewing, Stasi said, "Yes, I did, but he's always been respectful toward me. We're friends, sort of."

Rachel looked skeptically at Stasi as she slurped her soft drink. "Mmm-hmm."

"Stop looking at me like that!"

"Like what? I'm not looking at you any way at all."

"Uh-huh, sure."

Rachel leaned forward and placed her glass on the table. "Look, just be careful."

Dabbing her mouth with a napkin, Stasi looked at her friend incredulously. "Careful of what? I'm hardly in danger from a man lying paralyzed in a hospital bed."

Rachel plunked her fork onto her plate, and several people looked over at the crashing sound it produced. "I'm not talking about that, and you know it! I'm talking about your heart."

"Believe me, my heart was never in any danger from Slade Mitchell in the first place. In the second place, he already has a girl-friend. And in the third place, I'm not so insensitive as to think along those lines at a time like this! All I want to do right now is help him."

"Hey, you set me straight!" Rachel said, raising her palms in surrender. "But you're praying for him, aren't you?"

"Sure, all the time."

"Then I think that's all you can do at the moment."

Stasi nodded in agreement. "Yes, I'm afraid that *is* all I can do."

Stasi visited Slade that afternoon. When she first arrived, he appeared to be sleeping, so she decided to kneel by the side of his bed and bow her head in prayer. It was some minutes when his voice startled her.

"Don't waste your prayers on me."

Caught off guard, she lifted her head and immediately got to her feet. "I'm not. I mean. . . well, prayers are never a waste."

"They are on me."

Assuming the doctor relayed his uncertainty as to the extent of Slade's recovery, she empathized with him. Smoothing the hair off of his forehead, she said, "No, Slade, they're not. God loves you." When he didn't respond to this she changed the subject. "So tell me, have they tried to get you moving today?"

"Yeah, some physical therapist came in and tried to sit me up."

"Oh, that's terrific!"

"No, not terrific. I puked all over his shoes."

"Oh, well," she patted his arm. "You have to take things one step at a time."

Obviously seeing the movement in his peripheral vision, Slade looked down at his arm. "You know I can't feel that?"

How insensitive of her! Why didn't she think before she acted? "Yes. Yes, I know. I'm sorry."

"Don't be. It was a natural reaction."

She stood looking down at him, a pale, frail shell of the man she once viewed as strong, both physically and emotionally. He seemed to be at the breaking point. Then, an unexpected notion came to mind, which she immediately decided to relay to Slade.

"Slade, I know you may not want to hear this right now, but turning your problems over to God might help a great deal."

He stared at her, his eyes stormy, as if dark clouds had moved in overhead. "No." She began to protest, but he stopped her as he went on in a tight voice. "Where was *God* when my mother was shafted by the only man she ever loved and left on her own to raise his child? Where was *God* when I was a boy living in Camden and thought the only way to avoid beatings from gang members was to join them, only to find out it wasn't true? Where was *God* when I was dropping to an almost certain death?"

Understanding his pain, she felt tears spring to her eyes. It seemed he'd had a rough childhood and was bitter about it. She had never imagined anything like that happening to him. "But you survived all that. And you didn't die in that fall," she said in a small voice.

"No, I didn't. But that was just luck, if you can call it that. God didn't do that for me. He never did anything for me. Everything I ever accomplished I did on my own. Everything I own I acquired myself. Everything I am today was through my own efforts, not God's. I don't need God, and I don't need you, and your prayers, and your lectures, so GET OUT!"

"But . . . "

"I SAID GET OUT! NOW! AND DON'T COME BACK!"

Swiping at her tears, Stasi turned and walked toward the door, but before walking through it for the last time, she spun back around. "Before I go, there are some things you should know." She sniffed and pulled a tissue from her purse. "None of us can do anything without God. But Slade, you are a broken man right now. Times of brokenness are when God most wants us to come to Him. It brings us closer to Him. I just hope that someday you'll realize how much you need Him."

Turning slowly, she walked from the room. A little ways down the hall, she stopped and slumped against the wall to quietly weep for a lost soul and a lost friendship.

CHAPTER THIRTEEN

NOW THAT SLADE COULD STAY UPRIGHT WITHOUT VOMITING, the doctor had had him start on physical therapy and occupational therapy. The P.T., of course, was for strength, endurance, and possible recovery, or partial recovery, of the use of his limbs. The O.T. was a sort of training for adjusting to the everyday life of an invalid.

Invalid. That was how Slade thought of himself now. Not a valid human being, but canceled out. His body just a shell for the real man on the inside looking out at the world through the windows of his eyes.

His physical therapist, Marty Greenly, never referred to any of the patients as invalids. He used sugar-coated words like "physically challenged," as if he thought of the situation as some sort of sports competition. But Slade knew what he was, and he knew what he wasn't. Certainly not a whole man. Stasi had said he was a broken man. Right—broken and can't be fixed.

At first, Slade wanted no part of the therapy. He believed that the feeling in his limbs would miraculously return any day now. But then, after a few days of lying motionless in the hospital bed, he couldn't stand it. He was bored beyond belief and thought it a good way to kill time until he was discharged from the hospital.

After about a week of lying on a table while Marty pushed and pulled his limbs every which way, Slade graduated to the double bars.

"Okay, Slade, you don't have to do anything but stand at first," Marty told him. He helped Slade up out of the wheelchair and positioned him between the two bars at one end. When he let go, Slade's legs immediately folded under the weight, but Marty caught him before he reached the floor. This would not have been an easy task for most people, but Marty was a big man. Not taller than Slade, but broader and more muscular.

Slade stared with envy at Marty's bulging biceps and remembered when he had looked that good. Now, by lying in a hospital bed all these weeks, his muscles had begun to diminish.

"This is ridiculous! I feel like an infant."

"C'mon, buddy, you can do it. We'll take it one step at a time," Marty encouraged. "I'll support you."

"Do you think I'll ever be able to walk again, Marty?"

"That's not for me to say, Slade." He stood beside the bars and put one arm around Slade's ribcage. "Just stand here for a minute until you get your bearings." As he waited, he continued. "I will say that there are people who are told they may never be able to walk again, and I've seen them walk right out the hospital doors. On the other hand, some can only walk very little and need wheelchairs most of the time. And then there are others who can't even stand, let alone walk."

"I wonder which of those I'll be," Slade said.

"I don't know, man, but if you just push it to the limit, you'll know when you get there."

"Well, here I am, standing. What next?"

"Try taking a step."

Slade tried to lift his right foot and push it forward with all his might, even willed it to move. When he finally got it to move, it only dragged about two inches, but the effort made him perspire. To him, it felt like moving a five-hundred-pound sledgehammer.

"Okay, now see if you can do the same with the other," Marty instructed.

It took all of Slade's concentration and what was left of his stamina to move the left foot even a fraction of an inch, leaving him breathless and weak.

Neither of these feats was possible without Marty's physical support, Slade realized.

"That's enough for today," Marty said. "We'll try again tomorrow." He helped Slade back into the wheelchair, then mopped Slade's brow with a soft cloth.

When Slade's breath returned, he said, "I can't do it, Marty. I thought it was bad enough that the right foot only moved two inches, but when the left foot barely moved at all . . ." He closed his eyes, shaking his head.

"Now look, Slade. Granted those feet didn't go far, but they *did* move. That's progress! You'll do better each day. You'll see."

Too tired to argue, Slade just sat slumped into the chair. "Whatever you say."

"Next week we'll start working with weights, too," Marty cheerfully informed him while wheeling him back to his room.

"I can hardly wait," Slade deadpanned.

CHAPTER FOURTEEN

FIVE WEEKS HAD PASSED SINCE THE DAY THAT SLADE HAD thrown Stasi out of his hospital room. She still prayed for him every day but often found herself wondering how he was progressing. A few times she called the hospital, but they couldn't give her many details. Once, she even went so far as to venture a visit to the hospital, peeking through the window on the door to the physical therapy room to watch Slade for a few minutes as he worked with weights.

She had brightened at the sight that greeted her that day. The room was teeming with activity. People were exercising on all sorts of contraptions, she noticed as her eyes scanned the room until they came to rest on Slade and his therapist off in a corner on the right. His side was facing her, but he was positioned in such a way that to be able to see her, he would have to twist his head approximately one hundred thirty degrees. So she felt safe in watching him without being discovered.

He looked extremely better than the last time she'd seen him. His color had returned, and she could see no scars from this distance. The therapist handed him a small dumbbell, support-ing it while Slade lifted it, curling his arm at the elbow slowly and repeatedly. Slade wore a short-sleeved, navy blue tee shirt, and Stasi could see the ripple of his muscles beneath and below the sleeve as he worked. She was spellbound, not expecting this much progress in so short a time. Granted, it wasn't much weight, and he needed help, but it was an indication that the feeling in his hands and arms was returning.

Sighing with relief that things seemed to be going well for Slade, she turned away from the door and almost collided with Dr. Blanchard.

"Stasi, hello!"

"Hello, Dr. Blanchard."

"Where have you been? We haven't seen you around in a while."

"Oh, well, . . . Slade and I had a falling out over a month ago. That's the last time I was here."

"Glad to see you've made up." The corners around his blue eyes crinkled as he smiled.

Stasi shook her head. "No, we haven't made up. He doesn't know I'm here. I was just concerned about his progress, but I see he's doing fairly well."

"Yes, he is. But I'm sorry about your disagreement. I rather thought you were good for Slade to have around."

She rolled her eyes. "He didn't think so. He still has Melissa, though."

Dr. Blanchard indicated with his arm that she should walk with him. "Maybe, but she hasn't been around very often lately. Any-way, I never thought that it was good for Slade to have her around."

"Why not?"

They stopped in front of the elevators. "She's not very strong. Instead of encouraging him, she whines and worries over whether he'll ever be able to walk normally or if he'll always need a wheelchair and if he'll ever be self-sufficient."

"Poor Slade. He doesn't need that."

"No. If only you could . . ." He let his request drift off meaningfully.

"Sorry, Doctor. I would love to visit Slade regularly, but he made it quite clear that he doesn't want me around."

"Too bad." He gave her shoulder a quick pat. "Gotta go. Maybe I'll see you around sometime." He started off down the corridor, then stopped and turned. "On second thought, maybe we could go out for coffee or lunch one day?"

Stasi was taken aback but said, "Uh, okay Sure, I'd like that."

"Great! I'll call you. The desk has your number." Then he swiftly turned and was gone.

That had happened a week ago. Now Stasi wondered how much more progress Slade had made since then.

Slade lay exhausted in the hospital bed, ready to drift off to sleep for the night. The time had flown by in the past month, what with all the activities they'd had him involved in around here. There were physical therapy, occupational therapy, speech therapy and visits from Dr. Blanchard to chart his progress. His mind was in a whirlwind most days trying to keep up. That was good, as far as he was concerned. It kept his mind off his loneliness.

He didn't have many visitors. Once in a while, one of his partners dropped in, or his secretary. Of course, there was John. He dropped in sometimes and called pretty often, always assuring Slade that everything at the office was fine and that his clients were being taken care of until his return.

And then there was Melissa. Why wasn't she here every night, or at least a few nights a week? She'd been to see him only a few times after the first week. He thought she cared for him, but apparently he was wrong. Even Stasi seemed to care about him more than Melissa.

Stasi.

Boy, had he blown that one, and now he was sorry. He really wasn't in his right mind when he threw her out of his room that day. She'd been to visit him more times in that first week than any of his other visitors put together in the past month. What was difficult for him to understand was why she should be so concerned about *him*. It was probably a Christian thing. They were all like that, weren't they? They cared about everybody, even people they didn't know. Even so, he found himself missing her concern for him, the way she made him keep himself in line—at least around *her*. She had a freshness and honesty about her that left much to be desired in others. But most of all, he missed that playful banter that flew so easily between them.

Just before sleep took him, he came to the conclusion that Stasi was probably better off not having to bother about him at all.

CHAPTER FIFTEEN

ARLENE BROCK SAT AT HER DESK AND WATCHED THE hustle and bustle of everyday business occurring all around her. Something didn't seem right. Everyone acted as if things were normal around here. Was it normal for her to have so little work to do that she took overflow work from the other secretaries? Was it normal that Slade's clients had been dispersed among the partners and the associate? Was it normal that no one seemed to visit Slade, or even ask *her* how he was doing? Didn't anyone care?

Then there was the other thing that kept cropping up in her mind. Slade's accident seemed to have happened so soon after he had voiced his suspicions of foul play in the office. Was it a coincidence? She knew Slade was an expert skydiver. The police didn't investigate much, just wrote it off as another accident. Apparently, they were used to its happening occasionally. Just last year the airport that Slade utilized for his outings had two accidental deaths during skydiving expeditions.

Maybe if she spoke to Slade about it on her next visit it wouldn't keep nagging at her.

Yes, that's what she would do.

Slade was elated. Melissa was visiting tonight, and he was going to show her what he'd recently accomplished. Thanks to physical therapy, some of the feeling had returned in his arms and hands—the right side more than the left. Then he worked with the occupational therapist to learn to do some of the things he'd always been able to do before. The normal, everyday things.

At first, he'd balked, feeling he had regressed to infancy, but he soon realized that he'd get nowhere if he didn't even try. Now he felt that Melissa would be pleased with his progress.

Sitting up with his dinner tray laid out on the bed table angled over his lap, he waited for her, not caring if the food got cold. His stomach lurched in anticipation when he heard the click-clack of Melissa's high heels reverberating through the hall outside his room. Melissa appeared at the door, impeccably dressed in a red tailored skirt suit. A whiff of floral scent floated past Slade's nostrils.

"Hello, honey," she greeted him.

"Hi."

Noticing the tray and his untouched food, she moved quickly toward him. "Why haven't you eaten? Don't you feel well?"

"I feel fine. Great, in fact. I waited for you because I wanted to show you something I learned today," he said, flashing a brilliant smile.

"Oh. Okay," Melissa answered, looking perplexed.

"Just pull that chair over next to the bed and watch."

She did as she was told and sat down, folding her hands in her lap like a schoolgirl, a faint, expectant smile on her lips.

"Okay, now watch." Slade slowly raised his right hand toward the table and reached for the fork next to the plate. Touching it, he tried to curl his fingers around it and missed. Trying again, he succeeded, then proceeded to lift it slowly toward the plate. Concentrating earnestly, willing his hand to do his bidding, he sunk the fork into the brown lump of meat on his plate and jiggled it until a morsel came loose. Slowly and steadily, he pierced the tidbit, carried it to his mouth, and deposited it. Grinning like a proud little boy, Slade gazed at her while he chewed and swallowed the meat.

Melissa stared back, wide-eyed.

"Well, what do you think?"

"I . . . uh . . . well . . . I think it's great! I'm excited for you." Somehow the excitement didn't reach her eyes. "But. . ."

"But what?"

"I-is that all?"

It took that one question—and one second—to dissolve his feelings of pride and excitement, leaving his ego as limp as a deflated balloon.

Stasi and Dr. Greg Blanchard met for lunch at Shoney's Restaurant in Washington Township. Stasi had no qualms about seeing Greg, because during their phone conversation the night he called, she discovered that he also was a follower of Christ.

After filling their plates at the salad bar, Greg and Stasi expected to enjoy some stimulating conversation while eating.

"So, what do you do for a living?" Greg asked her.

Stasi explained as briefly as possible about her information bureau business. When he responded with a nod and, "Oh, that's interesting," she knew they were in trouble.

Silence, except for the clinking of forks against their plates.

Finally, Stasi asked, "So, how's Slade doing?"

"He's doing quite well, actually. He's able to use his hands a little, feed himself, groom himself . . . you know, the usual everyday things."

"Usual for us, but for Slade I'd imagine they're pretty *un*usual at this point."

Greg stopped eating, tilted his head, and looked at her. "You're very perceptive."

She smiled and they both resumed eating.

Silence again.

"Uh, how long do you think before he's released?"

"I really couldn't say. It depends on Slade and how hard he pushes himself."

Stasi nodded, and they continued eating.

More silence.

"So, you run an information bureau?" Their burst of laughter rang out through the restaurant. "It's pretty sad when the only thing we have in common to talk about is Slade Mitchell."

"Uh-huh," she said, still chuckling.

Greg sobered. "There's no chemistry here, is there?"

"I really don't think so. I'm sorry, Greg."

"No need to be. It works both ways."

Stasi raised her eyebrows. "If I didn't know better, I'd be insulted."

"But you do know better."

She smiled. "Yes, I do."

"I do think, though, that there's chemistry for you elsewhere."

"Where? What do you mean?"

"Think about it. Who has been our main topic of conversation, today and always?"

Stasi's eyes widened. "Slade? You have to be kidding! He doesn't even want to see me anymore."

"I don't think he meant it."

"Even if he didn't, we're just friends."

Greg smiled. "That's what they all say."

"It's true. Besides, he isn't my type at all."

"Oh? And what *is* your type?"

"Not someone who parties his life away, drinks, and womanizes. That lifestyle is not for me."

"I know that, but things have changed for Slade now."

"Yes, but not in the way that makes it okay for me. Besides, he still wants nothing to do with me."

"I believe he'll come around in time. On both counts. Furthermore, I think he'll be lucky to have you waiting in the wings."

Indignant that he should find her so pathetic, she said, "Who says I'll be waiting in the wings?"

"Of course, that's entirely up to you."

That was a possibility that she didn't want to explore right now. "You seem to forget about Melissa."

Greg checked his watch. "As far as I can see, I don't think that'll last much longer." He dug in his pocket, pulled out his wallet.

Stasi grabbed her purse and stood up. "What makes you say that?"

"She's not around much." He placed some bills on the table and stood. "In my book, if you care for someone, you're with them as much as possible, especially in such extenuating circumstances."

On the way out the door, Stasi said, "I guess you're right."

"I know I am," Greg replied. "I also know that if *you* could, you'd be with Slade right now."

Stasi didn't reply to that, but after Greg uttered a quick "Be seein' ya" and pulled away in his green BMW, she was left standing alone to deal with the mixed feelings their conversation had stirred up.

Chapter Sixteen

ARLENE BROCK SAT NERVOUSLY IN THE WAITING AREA OF THE Williamstown Police Department. The urgent hubbub of the routine machinations going on around her only added to the intestinal havoc wreaking in her stomach.

Maybe she shouldn't be doing this. It was probably a crazy idea, but it had been bothering her for a long time. She had told no one, not even Slade, and it was a terrible burden to carry alone.

After her initial decision to discuss her suspicions with Slade, she changed her mind. Slade had other problems to deal with at present, and she didn't want to open another can of worms. Obviously, he had no recollection of the conversation they'd had in his office that day.

And what if she were wrong about the whole thing? It would start something that would have great impact on everyone connected with the firm. Irrevocable damage would be done.

But what if she were right? Then at least she could sleep at night knowing she had done her duty as a citizen and as Slade's friend and secretary. But *would* she sleep? No. She'd be worried about who was out there trying to kill Slade and the fact that it could be someone with whom she came in contact every day.

"Ms. Brock?"

The voice cut into her speculation, and she stood up. "Yes?"

A tall man with salt-and-pepper hair and neatly dressed in a navy suit stood before her, hand extended. "Hello, I'm Detective Larry Jessup. Follow me to my office and then you can tell me how I can help you."

They walked a short distance down the hall, and he stood aside and ushered her through an open door. The office was very small but neat.

Detective Jessup took a seat behind the desk and gestured for her to sit across from him in a tweed fabric chair. After Arlene perched herself on the edge of the seat, he peered at her expectantly. "Okay, shoot."

Arlene's jitters dissipated, and a short laugh escaped her lips. "That's funny, coming from a cop!"

Jessup smiled. "I aim to please. Now what's the problem?"

She took a deep breath. "Okay. I was told that you handled the investigation on the skydiving accident of Slade Mitchell back in July."

Detective Jessup nodded. "Yes. It wasn't very detailed. A fairly simple case. Open and shut. I remember because we don't have many skydiving accidents."

"Yes, well, I'm not so sure it was an accident."

The detective leaned forward over the desk. "Ms. Brock, are you telling me that you think someone tried to kill Mr. Mitchell?"

"I'm not sure, but I think it's something that should be looked into."

"Okay," Jessup began, adjusting his chair closer to the desk, "let's start at the beginning."

Arlene nodded, pulled herself up straight and slightly narrowed her eyes as if in deep concentration.

"What is your relationship to Mr. Mitchell?" Jessup asked, grabbing a legal pad and a pen.

"I'm his secretary at the financial management firm he co-owns."

"I see," he said as he scribbled on the pad. "And what makes you think someone tried to murder your boss?"

She flinched at the word *murder*. It was a word she had tried to avoid, though no matter how she looked at it or tried to downplay it, the meaning was still the same.

"Ms. Brock?" Jessup prompted.

Looking into his kind blue eyes, she knew she could hold back no longer. The entire story spewed from her lips. Beginning with the time Slade first came to her about the missing file, she elaborated on his suspicions, interjected with his expertise on skydiving, finally ending with the cavalier attitude of his partners and colleagues toward his absence from the office.

When Arlene was finished, Detective Jessup sat staring thoughtfully at the legal pad where he'd furiously scratched out extensive notes during her diatribe. Finally looking up, he asked, "Why hasn't Mr. Mitchell approached us himself?"

"He has what the doctors call retrograde amnesia, meaning that he can't remember anything for a certain period of time prior to the accident. For him, it's one or two months."

"I see." He rose from the chair. "All right, Ms. Brock. In light of the suspicions Mr. Mitchell had about fraudulent practices going on, we'll look into it. I can't promise that the case will be reopened, though, unless you or Mr. Mitchell can come up with something tangible."

Arlene stood, too. "Perhaps Slade knew something before the accident and didn't have a chance to report it."

"Yes, but with this retrograde amnesia, it will be difficult to pin-point."

"The doctors seem to think his memory will return in time."

"But, Ms. Brock, the question is, how *much* time?" he said, before leaving the office to have her statement typed up.

As she left the station, Arlene pondered the fact that she didn't feel better, as she had expected. In fact, she felt worse, as Detective Jessup's question had raised another, more urgent one: Would someone get to Slade before his memory returned?

CHAPTER SEVENTEEN

SLADE LAY IN BED WATCHING TELEVISION. NOT REALLY watching, just staring at the screen, but not seeing what was on it. It was nighttime and he was lonely. Melissa hardly ever visited anymore. He wasn't even sure he wanted her to. He didn't feel up to a relationship, right now. But yet . . . it would be nice to know she cared. That someone cared.

Snap out of it, Mitchell! You were never the type to wallow in self-pity.

But then, he had never been in this kind of predicament before.

The phone rang, screaming into the quiet stillness, and he jumped. Frustrated that it seemed to take forever to make his arm reach over and pick up the receiver, he worried that the caller would hang up before he could get to it. Fortunately, on the fourth ring, he got it and took another lifetime to bring it to his ear. "Hello?" He was breathless after expending so much effort.

"Slade?"

"Melissa? What's up?" She sounded strange.

"I need to talk to you."

He shuddered at the tone in her voice when she said it. "Sounds serious. Are you coming over tonight?"

"No. I . . . I can't get there tonight."

"Well, when would you like to talk?"

"Right now, if that's okay." Her voice was strained.

"Go ahead, I'm listening."

He heard her take a deep breath, hold it for a few seconds, then let it out. "I . . . I can't see you anymore."

The words seemed to shoot through the receiver like bullets, riddling his ear, then his brain. "Why not?" He was sure he already knew.

"I can't take it anymore, seeing you flat in that bed, never getting better."

"I *am* getting better."

"But you'll never be the same. Your whole life will revolve around a wheelchair. You'll never be able to do the things you used to do."

She probably didn't realize that she not only had plunged the knife deep into his heart but also was now twisting it. "Does any of that matter?" he asked, his voice stiff.

She sniffed. "I know it shouldn't, but it does. You're just not the same man I fell for," she ended in a small voice.

"Maybe not physically, but I'm still the same on the inside. You have to take me as I am."

Melissa was sobbing now. "I can't. There's too much to deal with."

Slade was more angry than hurt. "You could have at least had the courtesy to tell me to my face, Melissa. I'm glad I found out how shallow and cowardly you are before it was too late!" He slammed down the phone—as fast as his heavy arm would allow.

Sleep was a long time in coming.

Arlene appeared in his doorway the next morning to the minute at the start of visiting hours. He could see she wasn't her usual bright and cheerful self.

"Hello, Slade," she said, taking the chair at his bedside.

"Hi, Arlene. What's up? You look sort of peaked, and you have dark circles under your eyes. Lack of sleep?"

"Sort of." Pulling in a deep, calming breath, she straightened in the chair. "Look, Slade, I'll cut right to the chase. You don't remember, but about a week before your accident, you discovered something very disturbing."

He remained quiet a moment, searching his memory. "You're right, I don't remember anything like that. Do you know what it was?"

She sat forward, nodding. "Yes, we spoke about it briefly, and you were supposed to look into it. You thought that someone in the firm was embezzling money from clients."

He struggled to lean forward. "But how? Why?"

Arlene explained about Mrs. Haloran and the missing file.

Slade laid his head back against the pillows, releasing a forceful rush of breath. What next? First, the accident, not to mention the results, then Melissa, and now this. Could things get any worse?

"I can't believe it." He quickly raised his head and looked hopefully at Arlene. "Did I find out anything?"

"I really don't know. As I said, it was about a week before the accident, and you were supposed to look into it. I don't know if you ever had a chance, or if you did, how far you got. We never spoke of it after that."

"Does anyone else know?"

"I didn't tell anyone, but I'm not sure if you took anyone else into your confidence."

Slade gave his head a quick shake, then lay back, staring at the ceiling. "This is unbelievable."

"Slade, th . . . there's more."

He looked up to see her trembling. Licking her dry lips, she said, "I went to the police yesterday because I thought it was possible that the accident really wasn't an accident."

Apparently, things *could* get worse.

"You can't mean that!" He wanted to rake his fingers through his hair, but his mind was racing and his nerve impulses couldn't respond. "To think that someone in the firm is committing fraud is hard enough to believe, but . . . murder?

"Slade, it may not be true, I know, but it crossed my mind. Then it kept nagging and nagging at me until it mushroomed and I couldn't handle it alone anymore. I had to tell someone, but I don't trust anyone at the firm these days, so I went to the police. I think they'll be coming by to question you."

A sharp, short laugh burst from him. "They won't get very far."

"I know, I told them that. I guess they have to start somewhere."

Slade slowly lifted his hand to cover Arlene's where it lay on the edge of the bed. "Thanks for letting me know. At least I'll be prepared. But I also want to thank you for your concern. At least I know *someone* cares."

She patted his shoulder. "C'mon, cheer up! Lots of people care about you. You have lots of friends, and there's always Melissa."

The name struck a nerve, and he flinched. "You can forget about Melissa. *I'm* trying to."

"Oh, Slade." Her brow creased. "What happened?"

He told her about Melissa's phone call the night before and how angry he had been over it. Arlene sympathized and fussed for a while, then announced it was time for her to go. Before leaving, she said, "Don't worry, Slade. You still have me."

"I know, Arlene. Thanks."

That afternoon, Detective Jessup stopped by, bringing with him young Detective Frank Burns. They flashed their badges and introduced themselves, describing Arlene's visit with them and explaining the reason for theirs with Slade. The young detective took out a small notepad, flipped some pages, retrieved a pen from his inside jacket pocket, and held it poised over the pad, gazing at Slade expectantly.

Then came the questions. The questions Slade knew none of the answers to.

"I realize you remember nothing at this point, Mr. Mitchell, but perhaps talking about it will jog your memory," Jessup prompted.

Slade stared at him. This tall, impeccably dressed, *elegant* man certainly did not fit the description of a stereotypical hard-boiled detective. His partner, on the other hand, so extremely and laughably did that Slade would venture to assume that the young, red-haired, freckle-faced detective had contracted the "Columbo syndrome." Though the weather was mild, he wore a crinkled all-weather coat, and his hair was rumpled as if he had just rolled out of bed that morning, dressed, and left home without ever looking into a mirror. The cigar was conspicuously absent.

"I'll do my best, Detective, but I can't promise anything."

"That's all we ask, son," Jessup assured. "Now, as to the alleged fraud, can you remember anything at all you may have discovered?"

Slade shook his head. "Ever since my secretary left this morning, I've been racking my brain. I'm sorry, Detective, I can't remember a thing." He ended this on a strained high note.

"That's all right, I understand. Perhaps in time." He cleared his throat before going on. "Now, about your . . . accident. Do you remember anything having to do with that?"

Slade glanced at Burns, saw him scribbling furiously on the notepad, and wondered whether anything he'd said so far could possibly be noteworthy. His eyes slid back to Jessup, and he shook his head once again. "Sorry. I didn't even know why I was here until someone told me what had happened."

Jessup sighed. "Okay, look, Mr. Mitchell. We're going to run an investigation, but that means we'll be questioning the people who were with you on your skydiving excursion—Ms. Brock was good enough to supply us with those names. We'll also collaborate with the Voorhees Police Department regarding the fraud. That's their jurisdiction. Heck, we might even end up turning the whole thing over to the county prosecutor's office!"

"But Detective . . . Arlene . . . won't she be in danger? I mean if someone from the office is responsible and they find out she went to the police . . ."

"No need to worry about that. We won't make it known to any-one that she came to us. But there *is* a danger to you, Mr. Mitchell. I must advise you not to trust *anyone*."

"I understand, Detective Jessup, but surely you can't mean my oldest and closest friends."

"Mitchell, I mean anyone," Jessup said in a clipped tone. "In situations like this, you never know who your friends really are. We don't have the manpower, nor is there enough evidence just now to warrant putting a guard outside that door." He jerked his thumb in the direction of the hospital room door.

"That's okay, I'll be going home soon."

"We know," Detective Burns piped up. "That's one of the things that worries us."

CHAPTER EIGHTEEN

STASI WAS AT HER DESK PUTTING A REPORT TOGETHER FOR HER latest client when the phone rang. It was Greg.

"Stasi, I have some news about Slade that I thought might interest you."

At the sound of Slade's name her heart began thumping against her ribcage. "Go on, I'm listening."

"The police were in to see him. It seems that they're doing an investigation as to whether or not someone tried to murder him."

"Murder!" If she weren't already sitting, she'd have sunk into the nearest chair. "Oh, no, poor Slade! How is he taking it?"

"Not well. He's been snapping at everyone lately. Of course, it's understandable. His physical disability alone is enough to send anyone into a depression, but I'm afraid he has more things on his plate than he can handle."

Stasi made a quick decision. "I have to see him. It's time to let go of my pride and just do whatever I can for him."

"I was hoping you'd say that. He needs someone, and I still don't see a lot of Melissa around." Greg cleared his throat. "Speaking of his needing someone, did you ever find how to contact his mother? We've asked him countless times, but all he'll say is he doesn't want to burden anyone."

"No, I'm sorry. None of the neighbors that I asked knew about her."

"Okay, just wondering. I'll probably see you when you get here."

"Sure thing."

An hour later, Stasi poked her head into Slade's room, unsure whether she should breeze right in.

"Hi. Mind if I come in?" she asked, hearing the shakiness in her own voice.

Slade turned his head toward her and after a moment shrugged. "Why not?"

Stepping through the door, she tentatively approached the bed. She wouldn't insult him by asking how he felt. She could well imagine. Honesty was best. "I heard about the police investigation."

"Who told you?"

"Greg. Dr. Blanchard."

"*Greg*, is it? You're on a first-name basis with *my* doctor?"

"Well, we're . . . we're friends."

"And how did that come about?"

"It's a long story."

"I'm *obviously* not going anywhere," he spat.

"It's really none of . . ." She stopped herself. This was the worst time to lose her temper. And what kind of Christian witness would she be if she acted on her own anger? "Look, Slade," she said softly, "I don't want to argue with you. I came here to offer my friendship and support."

"I don't need it!"

Struggling to keep her anger in check, she took a deep, calming breath. "Yes, you do. There are a lot of things going on in your life right now. You need all the support you can get."

Slade sighed and turned his head away.

After a full two minutes of silence that seemed like hours, she asked, "Does Melissa know? About the investigation, I mean."

He whipped his head around so fast she was surprised it didn't cause whiplash. "I don't want to talk about Melissa!" he shouted.

"Have you seen her lately?"

"I said I don't want to discuss it," he ground out, jaws clenched.

Stasi sank into the bedside chair and hung her head. This wasn't how she envisioned this visit at all. Why was he always so difficult with her? Maybe she should give up.

The silence stretched. Then in a small voice he said, "Melissa's gone."

She raised her head. "What?"

"I said she's gone. She broke up with me. She can't handle the excess baggage. There! Satisfied?" He turned his head away again.

He sounded so broken. Her heart was heavy for him. "Oh, Slade, I'm so sorry. I didn't know." She took his hand.

Looking down at their joined hands, he said, "I can feel that a little, you know."

She smiled and nodded.

"Back to Melissa," he said resignedly. "She called me up one night and told me over the phone."

She looked into his eyes and tried to convey all her sorrow without words. It wouldn't do to say it over and over. Slade would not want anyone to pity him.

"It's not that I'm so broken up about losing Melissa specifically. It just makes me wonder if *anyone* could care for half a man."

Perturbation at Melissa coursed through her veins. For doing this to him. For robbing him of his confidence and sense of self-worth.

She leaned closer to him, still clasping his hand. "Oh, Slade, you're not any less of a man. This," she indicated his body with a sweep of her free hand, "is just a shell. Manhood or being whole isn't constituted by physical attributes but by what's inside. Here." She touched her hand to his chest, where his heart lay beneath.

"Fancy words aren't going to change it, Stasi. I'm still an invalid. No one finds that attractive. It'll keep people from getting to know the man inside. What woman could ever love . . . this?" He looked down the length of his body.

"Lots of women would," she soothed.

He shifted his eyes back to hers, gazing intensely at her. "Could *you*?"

She looked into his eyes, her own unwavering. She didn't even have to consider, and she answered him honestly. "Yes, I could, if he were the right man."

Slade turned away again. "You're just saying that to make me feel better."

He sounded like a child, but she would allow it for the moment, considering all he'd been through.

"Give me some credit. I think you know me better than that."

He turned back to her once again. "You're right. I'm sorry." He sighed. "Trouble is, there just aren't many women around like you."

Stasi's heart gave a little flutter at what he had just said. Somehow, having Slade think so highly of her made her feel good.

At that moment, Greg Blanchard strode in. "Hello, Slade." Then he stopped midstride when he spotted Stasi in the chair and moved toward her. "Stasi, hello!" He planted a loud smack on her cheek before she knew what was happening, and she peered up at him, astonished. Greg then stood behind her and placed a hand possessively upon each of her shoulders while she noticed the look that Slade shot them. Was it disgust? It certainly couldn't be jealousy.

Greg went to the foot of the bed and picked up Slade's chart. "Let's see how we are today." He pulled an approving expression as he studied it, then replaced it. "Everything looks good, as you know." He turned to Stasi. "Did Slade tell you that he's being released in a few days?"

"No, he didn't." Turning to Slade, she said, "That's terrific!"

"Yeah," he mumbled petulantly.

This new mood of his upset her, but she had to get back to work and told him so. "Perhaps I'll be back this evening," she added before leaving.

He brightened a little at that. "Sure, that would be nice."

She smiled and turned to go, but Slade's voice stopped her. "Stasi."

"Yes?"

"I'm sorry about how I acted earlier. And before, too. Will you forgive me?"

Feeling her smile broaden, she said, "You've already been forgiven."

Greg followed her from the room, and when they got far enough down the hall, she turned on him angrily. "What was that all about?"

"All what?" He was all innocence.

"That—that kiss! And the hands on my shoulders! Did you see the look Slade gave us?"

"Yes, I did, and I'd say it worked very well."

"What worked?"

"I was just trying to help things along, my girl." He sauntered on down the hall as Stasi gaped at his retreating form.

CHAPTER NINETEEN

IT WAS SUNDAY MORNING, AND SLADE WAS GOING HOME. HE had arranged for Arlene to pick him up from the hospital, but she had called and told him that Troy Kent *insisted* on having the honor of taking his good buddy home. Slade wondered why, if they were such "good buddies," he had hardly seen Troy during his hospital stay.

The mid-September day was sunny, warm, and breezy. As Slade was wheeled out to the car, he lifted his face to the sun, reveling in the rays soaking into his skin. It had been a long time.

Troy's black Acura Legend pulled into the parking lot of the Chestnut House Apartments, gliding into the closest spot he could find to the door. He removed Slade's wheelchair from the trunk and placed it by the passenger-side door so that Slade could ease his way over and into it. He had been shown how to do this in occupational therapy at the hospital.

While Troy retrieved the rest of his belongings from the car, Slade popped the front of his wheelchair up to make it over the small curb, then slowly but surely rolled himself to the entrance. He stopped, faced with the challenge of pulling open one of the double glass doors and wheeling himself through.

Seeing his dilemma, Troy hurried over to get the door, but Slade stopped him.

"No, Troy. I need to learn to do these things for myself."

Troy stepped aside. "Sure, pal, it's all yours."

Pulling along the door sideways, Slade reached for the handle and pulled while wheeling backward with his free hand. When there was enough space, he maneuvered the chair so that the footrests held the door while he wheeled through, keeping the door open alternately with his elbow and the chair itself.

He felt triumphant at handling such a task on his own. He had been warned that going through doors that had to be held open was one of the most difficult challenges for the wheelchair-bound.

They rode the elevator up to the second floor, and as they passed Stasi's apartment, Slade knew that she wouldn't be home. She spent practically the whole day and part of the evening at church.

When Slade let them into his apartment, Troy carried Slade's bag in. "Where would you like me to put this?"

"Oh, here." Slade wheeled over to him. "Place it on my lap, and I'll take it to my bedroom."

When Slade came out of the bedroom, Troy was nowhere in sight. "Troy?"

"Yeah?" came his voice from the other bedroom that Slade used as an office.

"What are you doing in there?"

He came out of the room looking, Slade thought, a little frustrated. "I was just checking around to see if things were accessible to you." He strolled over to the kitchen, looking up at the cabinets and opening one. "You might have trouble reaching things up there."

Slade wondered why Troy would think of something like that. But then, Troy was his friend and cared about him. Right? Besides, a lot of people acted differently around him now. Why should Troy be any different?

Then Detective Jessup's words came back to him. *Don't trust anyone. In situations like this, you never know who your friends are.* He shrugged off the thought. There was nothing in his office that Troy hadn't already seen.

"I'm going to head out, Slade. I have a lot of things to do today."

"Sure, Troy. And thanks for taking me home."

"No problem, buddy. See ya!" Then he was gone, and Slade spent the rest of the day reacquainting himself with his apartment and practicing maneuvers with his wheelchair.

At eight-fifteen that evening, Stasi knocked on Slade's door. At a muffled "door's open," she poked her head in. "I know I'm a little late, but I just thought I'd stop in to see if you needed anything."

Slade was just sitting in the middle of the room in his wheelchair. He seemed so bereft. "No, I'm fine."

"Have you eaten?" She now walked fully into the room.

"Yeah, I had a frozen dinner."

"A frozen dinner? We can't have that! I'll do some grocery shopping for you tomorrow."

"Thanks."

"Why don't you make a list of everything you need?"

"Okay, but later, if you don't mind. I'm not in the mood right now." He hadn't even looked at her the whole time they spoke.

"Sure. I'll pick it up tomorrow morning." She paused, groping for words to fill the awkward silence. Greg had warned her that Slade had mood swings and that it was fairly natural, considering the circumstances. "Is there anything else I can do for you, tonight or tomorrow?"

He suddenly lifted his head as if a lightbulb had flashed on above it. He turned the chair so that he could face her. "Come to think of it, there might be. If you're not too busy, that is."

"Well, ask and then we'll see."

"Would you have time to drive me to physical therapy tomorrow afternoon? I could take a cab, but at this point in time, I'd rather not."

She thought for a moment. "I think I can swing it." The least she could do was be there when he needed her. She'd take him to all his therapy sessions. "I'll do the grocery shopping first thing in the morning, shoot back here, and do some work until it's time to go. I could even take the laptop with me and do some work while I'm waiting for you."

"Sounds good. Thanks."

"No problem. What time are you scheduled for?"

"Two o'clock."

"Fine. How often do you go?"

"Every other day for several weeks, then it will taper off. I had extensive therapy during my hospital stay."

"Okay I think I can swing it."

He looked up at her, incredulous, then began wheeling toward her. "Stasi, I didn't mean. . ."

"She held up a hand to stop his protests. "I know, Slade. I just want to."

"You're sure?"

"Positive. I have to go, but I'll stop by at eight tomorrow morning for your shopping list." She moved toward the door.

"Thanks, Stasi. I'm really grateful for all your help."

"No problem, Slade," she said, walking out the door.

The next morning, Stasi showed up at Slade's apartment at eight o'clock sharp. When he handed her a computer-printed list, she realized with a jolt what a chore this must have been for him to prepare. No wonder he didn't want to bother while she had been there. She had forgotten that he couldn't just pick up a pen like he used to and scratch out anything he wanted in a matter of seconds. She silently berated herself for her unfeeling expectations. On the other hand, she knew he wouldn't want her to baby him by offering to do things for him that he should tackle on his own. He was the independent, determined type and wouldn't want anyone hovering over him for every little thing. But in the future, she would remember to be more sensitive to anything that may be an obstacle for him.

When she returned from the shopping trip, Slade announced that he had spent the time phone shopping and ordering a portable home gym to be set up in a corner of his office. "I'm determined to get back as much of myself as I possibly can," he added.

This seemed to be one of Slade's "good" days, and Stasi could see that he was almost his old self, character-wise. "I'm sure you'll do it, too," she encouraged as she put away the groceries.

Her car was parked a little ways down the lot, and next to it was Slade's silver Jag. He stopped the wheelchair and gazed at it longingly. Stasi's heart ripped apart at the look on his face. She knew how much he loved that car.

He turned to her as she opened the trunk of her Nissan. "Do you think I'll ever drive it again?"

She didn't want to blow this chance, so she answered him with a truthfulness from her heart. "With God, anything is possible."

Slade shook his head and wheeled over to the passenger side of Stasi's car. "Here we go," he mumbled. "Religious mumbo jumbo."

She let that remark slide and opened the door so he could ease himself out of the wheelchair and into the car. After Slade explained how to fold the chair, she lifted it into the trunk.

At the rehabilitation center in Marlton, Stasi had an hour to work on a report for one of her clients while she waited for Slade. When he met her in the waiting area afterward, he seemed in high spirits.

"You know, I always feel so tingly after therapy." He paused for a moment, apparently in thought, as Stasi wheeled him out to the car. "Maybe," he went on, "you're right about anything being possible—with or without God."

She didn't want to get into it with him about this conflicting statement, so instead she asked, "How do you mean?"

"I think there's a chance that if I really put my mind to it and try hard, I could go pretty far. Maybe I *will* drive the Jag again."

She just couldn't let that go by. She had to say something. After all, doesn't God want us to spread His Word? "Slade, you *can* do it, but only God is in control of our lives, not us. You can't do it alone. You need Him. We all need Him."

"Stasi, please, let's not spoil this moment. I don't have many of them."

She didn't answer but instead let out a long, frustrated sigh.

CHAPTER TWENTY

DETECTIVE JESSUP WAS STYMIED. SITTING AT HIS DESK, HE pored over his notes from an interview with one of the skydiving instructors at Skydive Heaven, where Slade did his jumping. Thankfully, what was left of Slade's parachute had still been in the evidence room. After examining it, he wanted answers to some questions. First, when he asked the instructor to show and explain an intact chute to him, he realized that the throw-out ball—or "hackey sack," as the instructor called it—and the cut-away cord were not attached to Slade's chute. He wondered why and how. Secondly, he assumed that there would be some type of gear check before anyone would be allowed to jump. And thirdly, why hadn't the duty officer obtained the answers to these questions in the first place?

Actually, he had his answer to the last question right in front of him on the police report. The chute was so tattered that it was assumed that any damage to it occurred during the course of the accident when Slade plummeted through the tree.

As for the two severed cords, the instructor confirmed that yes, it could have happened the way the report stated, so he could not fault the officer who made the report. But on closer inspection of the actual chute, Jessup found that the cords were cut clean. If they had been ripped off during the accident, they would have been somewhat shredded.

Concerning a gear check, the instructor informed Jessup that since the chute was Slade's property and not the establishment's, they were not responsible. They only did the checks on their own equipment. He further stated that anyone owning his own equipment might not feel that a gear check is necessary, since he most likely packed it himself.

So where did that leave Jessup? Questioning Slade's skydiving cronies, that's where. He rubbed his forehead in frustration, fervently wishing that Slade's memory would return.

Returning from a trip to the post office, Stasi was about to let herself into her apartment when she was startled by a sharp cry and the sound of glass crashing, followed by some colorful expletives that caused her to cringe. The sounds came from the direction of Slade's apartment.

Hurrying to the door across the hall, Stasi knocked, didn't wait for an answer, and burst in. She found Slade on the kitchen floor among scattered shards of glass, his wheelchair a few feet away.

"Slade! What happened?" She rushed over, grabbed the wheelchair, and pushed it closer, then helped him into it.

"I hoisted myself to reach for a glass in the cabinet." His voice was laden with bitterness. "As I let myself back into the chair, it wheeled back. I forgot to put on the brake," he added woefully.

"Are you cut or hurt in any way?" she asked, looking him over.

"Just my pride."

She pushed him into the living room. "They have special aids for things like reaching high items and such, you know."

"I know, but I wanted to do everything I could the normal way." He shook his head. "I'll never get used to this thing!" he growled through clenched teeth.

"Come on, now, it's not *that* bad. At least you didn't get cut." He jerked his head and glared at her, but she hurried on before he could pounce on that last statement. "Where's the broom and dustpan? I'll sweep up the glass."

He pointed to the closet.

After she had finished cleaning up, Stasi noticed the uncapped bottle set out on the kitchen counter half filled with amber liquid. She quietly recapped it and put it in an overhead cabinet, heart-heavy with the knowledge that Slade relied on alcohol to get him through these rough times.

Moving to the couch beside where Slade's wheelchair was parked, Stasi plopped herself down. "Well," she began lightly, "looks like you'll have to perfect your technique."

"I'm glad you can find humor in my misfortune," he snapped. "You don't understand what it's like to have had everything one day, and then suddenly, the next, it's all gone."

She tried hard to hold back the anger, but couldn't. "I can't pretend to understand how you're feeling right now, but I *can* understand what it's like to lose all that makes you happy." She sat forward now. "I finally realized I had to swallow my pride, stop feeling sorry for myself, and move on!"

Once it was out, she wanted to snatch it back. The cumbersome words hung suspended between them, and the ensuing silence crackled with tension.

"I'm awfully sorry, Slade," she said softly. "That was insensitive of me."

"You're crazy, you know that?" He flung the words at her in rebuff.

"I've been called worse." She recalled the deserved insults that Barry's mother had hurled in her face the day of his funeral.

More silence.

"What happened?" His voice was quiet. The mood had passed.

"Happened?"

"You know. The thing that made you feel sorry for yourself. If you don't mind my asking."

"No, I don't mind." She looked down at her hands, twiddled her fingers, figuring she'd tell him as much as she could. "Three years ago, I was engaged to be married." Without looking, she knew Slade gave a start. She'd never spoken of it with him or anyone else since it happened. Tucking her hair behind her ears, she continued. "We were college sweethearts, just graduated. Everything was in place for the wonderful life ahead: We both had great careers to look forward to, we had each other, and our families approved. What more was there to want?"

She paused, and Slade took the chance to jump in. "What happened? Obviously you didn't marry him."

"It was late winter, a few months before the wedding. Barry was on his way over to my apartment that night. There had been an ice storm a few days before, and everything was beginning to thaw, and since we hadn't been able to see each other for three days, I was anxious for him to visit. One of the roads along the way had a sharp bend. As he came around it, the car swerved, hit a patch of ice, and skidded out of control. He ended up going off the road and crashing into a tree." Quaking on the inside, she knew she couldn't relay all of the details. Not yet. If she did, he may never want to see or speak to her again.

Slade reached over and placed a comforting hand on her shoulder. "Oh, Stasi, I'm so sorry."

Sniffing and dabbing under her eyes with her fingers, she smiled tremulously. "There was a witness to the accident who told the police that the car went off the road because he tried to avoid hitting a small animal that darted out in front of him. It was dark, but they thought it was probably a cat."

Seeming a little uncomfortable, Slade mumbled, "He must have been a very caring person to give his life for a cat."

"Oh, he was!" she said, smiling and swiping the wetness from her cheeks. "He cared about everyone and everything. That's one of the things I loved about him." She averted her eyes and shrugged. "Anyway, it kind of makes you a little afraid to give your heart away again. You just never know when it will be crushed."

Slade nodded with a far-off look. "Yeah, you never know," he responded. Stasi could tell he was remembering how his had been so recently crushed by Melissa. "You know, it makes a person wonder, though."

"About what?"

"For instance, you trust God so implicitly. How can He let these things happen to someone like you? Or to your fiancé?"

She hesitated a moment. This question was always a tough one to answer. "No one understands His ways, Slade." Recalling her part in the whole thing, she continued. "I didn't know Him back then. He doesn't stop us from making the choices we make, but He uses adversity to reveal things about us that will bring us closer to Him. Everything that happens to us, good or bad, is used for the good. He always works things out perfectly."

Slade frowned at her skeptically. "Does it seem perfect to you that your fiancé was killed? That you lost someone you loved?"

"Right now, I can't honestly say it does. But we can't always see the big picture. We may never know for what purpose God allows things to happen until we meet Him face-to-face."

Slade shook his head. "That unshakable faith of yours. I don't think I could ever attain it."

CHAPTER TWENTY-ONE

"I WISH WE HAD A LITTLE MORE TO GO ON," FRANK BURNS said. "I don't like going in on the blind like this."

"I don't much like it myself, Frank, but if we keep digging, something's bound to come out of it either way."

Jessup steered the gray sedan into a parking slot in front of the Main Street office building where Conrad, Mitchell, Kent, and Schriver was located and cut the engine. He turned and looked at his partner. "Ready, Frank?"

Frank pulled his trusty pen and pad from his inside coat pocket. "As ready as I'll ever be, Larry."

Jessup rolled his eyes. He knew that people pegged Frank for an eccentric, bungling idiot. But Frank wanted it that way. If people knew how observant he really was, they wouldn't as readily let their guard down. The sad part was that even though Frank was as sharp as a tack and essential to an investigation, he remained in the background while Jessup asked all the questions, and people often gave Jessup all the credit when the pair solved a case. But Frank didn't mind at all. In fact, he wanted it that way. Notoriety was not something he strived for. All he wanted was to do his job and go home to his wife and kids at the end of the day.

Larry, on the other hand, welcomed all the hoopla and commendation. His job was his life, because he had none outside of his work. At fifty-three, he was divorced, and his kids had grown, gotten married, and moved away. His only thrill nowadays came from that elation related to solving a big case, or even a small one, for that matter.

The two men entered the building and took the elevator to the third floor. Upon entering the office, Jessup noticed Arlene Brock at one of the desks on the far side of the room but gave no indication he was acquainted with her. Instead, he and Frank moved toward the receptionist's desk and displayed their badges.

"We're from the Williamstown Police Department," Larry told the stunned young receptionist, who stared dazedly at the badges. "I'm Detective Larry Jessup, and this is Detective Frank Burns," he continued, gesturing toward Frank.

"H-how may I help you?" the young woman stammered.

"We'd like to speak with some of the partners. . ."

"Is there a problem I can help you gentlemen with?" John Conrad's voice rang out from a small alcove, and the receptionist looked relieved to see him. He extended his hand. "I'm John Conrad, senior partner of this firm."

Jessup shook his hand. "The name's Larry Jessup, from the Williamstown Police Department," he said, flashing his badge for the second time in less than five minutes. He thumbed toward Frank. "This is my partner, Frank Burns. May we speak with you privately?"

"Of course. Follow me." John led them down a long hallway and walked through the door at the end of it. A woman with short, blonde hair looked up from her desk, and John said, "Hold all my calls, Donna," as he strode into an inner office.

John settled into his plush velour chair and indicated that the detectives sit in the two burgundy leather wing chairs in front of his desk. "What seems to be the problem?" he asked after they were settled.

Larry cleared his throat. "We're considering reopening the case of Slade Mitchell's accident that occurred some months back, and we'd like to speak to the men who were with him the day it happened."

John looked thoughtful for a moment. "I hadn't realized that there even was a 'case,' but may I ask why?"

"There seems to be some question as to what really happened," Jessup explained.

"And who is raising the question, Detective?"

"I'm not at liberty to say, Mr. Conrad."

John nodded. "Of course. My secretary will fetch each of the men for you, and you can use the conference room at the other end of the hall. I can't speak for the men as to how cooperative they'll be. This is a busy time of the day, and I'm not sure if any of them will be available. I'm assuming this isn't a formal interrogation?"

"At this point, no. Right now we just need everyone's account of what happened," Jessup said.

"All right. Good luck, gentlemen."

They all shook hands, and then Larry and Frank left the office for the conference room while John gave instructions to his secretary.

The first to be questioned was Clark Schriver. The two detectives had him sit in the chair at the head of the long conference table.

Jessup paced around the room in total silence before starting the questioning. He always did this purposely because it helped him to determine whether a suspect had something to hide by the way he acted as he waited for him to begin. With a quick glance, he noticed the shine on Clark's forehead. Since the room was air conditioned, he knew that it wasn't because of the heat.

He stopped pacing and stood beside Clark's chair, leaning close and bracing his hands on the conference table. "Tell us everything that you know happened the day that Slade Mitchell was almost killed while skydiving." He knew his nearness made the man nervous.

Clark looked up at him. "Just while we were in the air, or from the beginning?"

"From the beginning."

"Okay. Well . . ." Clark's eyes roamed around the room as he thought, and he twisted his watchband in circles around his wrist. "When Slade and Troy arrived at the drop zone, a load of divers was waiting to go up, and they had barely made it in time."

"Who all was waiting to go up?"

"Darrell Boyd and I. The rest were people we didn't know."

Jessup heard Frank's pen scratching on his notepad. "I see. So then what?"

"Well," he shifted his eyes around, "to get on that plane before it left, Darrell and I helped Troy and Slade on with their gear."

Jessup took a chair at the table to the left of Clark. "And which of them did *you* help, Mr. Schriver?"

Clark turned his watchband. "S-Slade."

"Go on."

"We went up in the plane, then when it reached the required altitude, we all jumped out."

"Did Slade jump before or after you?"

He moved his eyes around the room again. "Uh, I think it was before."

"So, he would have been below you during the descent?"

"That's correct."

Jessup leaned forward. "So what did you see?"

Clark swallowed. "When we all deployed our chutes, it naturally slowed our progression. All except for Slade. He shot right past everyone without his chute up."

"Did you see him try to deploy his chute?"

"No. I wasn't really paying attention. Then I heard people shouting, and when I looked down, he was falling fast. From my viewpoint, he was about the size of a large ant when I saw his reserve chute engage, but it didn't open fully because the main canopy was still attached."

"What were you thinking at that time?"

His eyes roamed the room again. "It happened so fast, I wasn't sure what to think. I do remember wondering why he didn't pull the cutaway handle."

Jessup stood, began pacing again. "So then what happened?"

Clark closed his eyes, brows furrowed as if the memory were painful. "He disappeared from sight," he whispered.

Jessup allowed a deliberate pregnant pause and was grateful that Frank's pen stopped scribbling. Frank knew the drill. Coming to stand beside Clark's chair, he asked, "Is there anything else?"

"All I know is that when we all reached the ground, Slade was hanging in a tree and people were trying to get him down."

"All right, Mr. Schriver, that will be all." Clark stood, and Larry shook his hand. "Thank you for your cooperation."

A few minutes later, Troy Kent was seated in the chair that Clark had vacated. Jessup used the same pacing technique he'd used on Clark, only Troy didn't break out into a sweat. He possessed a calculated calmness.

When Jessup returned to Troy's end of the table and sat down, he asked, "You're one of Mr. Mitchell's best friends, aren't you, Mr. Kent?"

"Yes, sir."

"So you must have been devastated by the incident."

"Yes, sir." His eyes met Larry's dead on, but they showed no emotion.

"Okay, so tell us what happened on the day in question, from the beginning."

"I've already told the police the first time, but if I must . . ." He sighed and shifted in the chair. "I picked Slade up for our outing," he began in a monotone. "We were a little late arriving at the drop zone, so Clark and Darrell helped us into our gear and then we hurried onto the plane . . ."

"Hold it a moment, Mr. Kent. Why were you late to the airport?"

Troy thought a moment. "I really have no idea. Maybe the plane was going up a few minutes earlier than usual. Or maybe it was because I had to rearrange a few things in my trunk to fit Slade's gear in. Or maybe both."

Jessup considered Troy's answer for a moment. "Okay, Mr. Kent, go on."

"After we all jumped out and pulled our hackey sacks, I noticed Slade fly right by me and continue falling until he was out of sight."

"So then you jumped out of the plane before he did?"

"Yes, sir."

"Did you see him try to deploy his chute after he passed you?"

"No, sir."

Jessup stood and said, "Okay, Mr. Kent, you may go now. Thank you."

Troy left the room without a word.

"There's something about that guy, Larry," Frank said as they waited for Darrell Boyd to come in.

"I know what you mean."

Darrell appeared, and Frank indicated the same chair where the others had sat.

Something told Larry he did not need to use the pacing technique with this man. His face seemed kind and open.

Bracing one foot on the edge of the table and leaning on his knee with crossed arms, Larry asked, "Are you and Slade Mitchell good friends?"

"No, sir," Darrell answered without hesitation.

"Good enough to go skydiving with, though."

"Well, I'm afraid that Slade Mitchell only tolerates my presence."

Jessup sat down. "Why is that, Mr. Boyd?"

Before answering, Darrell glanced at Frank as he scribbled in his notebook. "I was up for a partnership, but Slade nixed it. There's been some tension between us since then."

"I see." Jessup contemplated this for a moment. "So tell us what happened the day of the skydiving accident.

"When Troy and Slade arrived at the airport, we were waiting to go up, so we hurried them up by helping them with their gear."

"Which of the men did *you* help, Mr. Boyd?"

"Troy."

"Okay. Then what?"

"On the plane, I noticed that part of Slade's pilot chute was sticking out of his pack and asked him if he wanted me to stuff it back in. He said okay, and I did. Then we all jumped out. After we opened our chutes, I noticed that Slade's wasn't open, because he kept falling real fast! As I watched him drop, I thought I saw a partial deployment, but then he was gone from my sight." He sadly shook his head at the memory.

"Is that everything?"

"Yes, except that the next thing I knew we were all at the hospital, waiting for news."

Jessup stood up, once again. Shaking Darrell's hand, he said, "Thank you, Mr. Boyd. You may go."

Minutes later, Larry and Frank were in the car, driving back to the station.

"So what do you think?" Frank asked.

"Hard to say at this point. What do you have in your notes?"

Frank flipped through the pages of his notepad. "Clark Schriver seemed sort of nervous. His eyes darted around a lot, he continually rotated his watchband—a Rolex, I might add—and his forehead broke out into a sweat."

"Yeah, but that could be attributed to the fact that he was being questioned by the police. You know how anxious people are around the police, even if they have nothing to hide."

Frank nodded.

"What else you got?" Larry asked, flipping on the right-turn signal and slowing the car to take the corner.

"Next we have Troy Kent. Man, but he was a cool customer, wasn't he?"

"I suspect he's always that way. Sometimes that's the way you have to be to succeed in this world."

"But the way he told his story was sort of mechanical. Like he'd been rehearsing it."

"He had plenty of time to do that before it was his turn. He wasn't taken by surprise like the first guy."

Frank shook his head. "You have an answer for everything, Larry."

"I like to knock you down every chance I get." His voice held an affectionate note. Frank was the best partner he'd ever had. They clicked. They could insult each other to the hilt but still maintain a special closeness, just like Laurel and Hardy or Abbott and Costello. "Okay, tell me what you think of Darrell Boyd."

"Not much to tell. He admitted his hard feelings toward Mitchell since Mitchell shot down his chance at a partnership. If he had tried to murder him, would he have given us his motive?"

Larry raised his eyebrows in contemplation.

"On the other hand," Frank continued, "he could be using that as a means of diverting our suspicions."

"So basically, Frank, none of that clears any of them, nor does it point the finger at any of them."

"That's about it, Larry. They all had their hands on Slade Mitchell's parachute before the jump. They're all suspects until it can be proven otherwise. Furthermore, I think we have to consider the fact that it could have been a conspiracy. Especially if what Ms. Brock told us checks out."

"So, we're right back where we started."

"It sure looks that way, Larry."

Chapter Twenty-Two

"I DON'T LIKE THIS," THE MAN HISSED INTO THE PHONE. "WHY, after all these months, are they reopening the case?"

"Somebody knows something. Went to the police," the other party speculated. "And that means that either Mitchell remembers something or he told someone else before this all happened and they're putting two and two together."

"I told you you should have finished him from the beginning!"

"You just hold on!" The other man shouted, then lowered his voice as if he just realized he could be overheard. "You should have done it yourself if you thought you could do a better job."

"I've already explained why I couldn't do it."

"Then don't complain. I did the best I could. I told you I didn't like it, anyway."

"Would you like prison better?"

A moment of silence. His instincts always proved right when it came to which buttons to push. Some people were so weak.

"You know I wouldn't, but murder . . ."

"It has to be done. And soon."

CHAPTER TWENTY-THREE

ON TUESDAY, STASI SPENT THE MORNING WORKING ON HER laptop at Slade's apartment. They had somehow come to an unspoken understanding in their friendship that allowed them to spend time together in companionable silence or engaging in lively conversation.

Stasi sat at Slade's desk while Slade worked out on the portable gym. The clicking of computer keys and the "swish-hiss" of the weight pulleys invaded the morning serenity. The sounds of progress.

"Shall I get you a drink?" she asked, keeping her eyes on the monitor.

"That would be good," Slade forced out with effort, continuing his exercise. "I'm almost finished with this set."

Stasi went out into the kitchen, retrieved two bottles of water from the refrigerator, and carried them back to the office. "Here you go."

He took the bottle she held out to him. "Thanks."

Sinking back into the chair, she watched Slade guzzle his water while she took prim, tiny sips of hers. He was getting stronger. In fact, his arms seemed more powerful than they had ever been, though she knew that some of the sensation would never return. During one of his more agreeable moments, she had asked him to describe how it felt. Smiling inwardly, she recalled his use of the word *rubbery.*

"What?"

Her eyes came into focus as she was yanked from the land of cogitation. "Hmm?"

Slade wiped his face with the towel that had been draped around his neck. "You were staring at me."

"No, I wasn't."

"Yes, you were."

Placing the water bottle on the desk, she said in a mock haughty tone, "Don't flatter yourself. It may have *looked* like I was staring at you, but in truth, my thoughts were somewhere else."

Slade shrugged his magnificent, glistening shoulders. "Okay. I suppose you wouldn't tell me what you were thinking about?"

"You suppose right."

A mischievous grin spread across his lips. "You can't fault a guy for trying."

"I guess not, but seriously, I *have* been thinking about something else I'd like to tell you." Slade looked at her, his eyes questioning. She stood up and began pacing around the small room. She had removed her sneakers, and her stockinged feet made soft padding sounds on the carpet. "I'm worried about the danger you may be in. Aren't you?"

Shaking his head and shrugging, he answered, "Not much, really. Since there haven't been any other incidents, I'm hoping that Arlene and the police are wrong."

She stopped pacing. "But shouldn't we be doing something?"

"Like?"

Shaking her head with quick jerks and casting her eyes about the room, she foraged for an answer. "I don't know," she blurted.

Slade reached for the nearby wheelchair and heaved himself into it. "Then you're in good company. Neither do I." He pulled up each leg to position his feet on the footrests. "Without any recollection of what I may have found out before the accident, there isn't nearly enough evidence for Jessup and Burns to build a case."

Stasi heaved a troubled sigh. "I know. Maybe we should search your office."

Slade squinted, appearing in deep contemplation. "It might be worth a try, but it would be dangerous. And someone may have already beaten us to it."

"It wouldn't be so dangerous if we went late at night after everyone was gone. I'm sure you have a key to the building."

"Yes, I have one."

"Good. C'mon." She strode out the door into the living room.

Wheeling out behind her, he asked, "Where?"

"In here, so we can sit and plan our strategy."

Pulling alongside the overstuffed chair that Stasi had plopped onto, Slade seemed pensive.

"What's wrong?" she asked him.

He propped his elbows on the armrests and laced his fingers. "You've been using the words *we* and *our* through this whole conversation. I don't think you should involve yourself in this."

"Oh, c'mon, Slade. We're friends. I'm here for you. I want to help."

"But why would you . . ." He stopped himself when she shot him a fierce, reproving glare. Bobbing his head slowly, he remembered. "Oh, yeah, I forgot. It's a Christian thing."

Rolling her eyes, she admonished, "Oh, Slade! It's that, and so much more! But, yes, coming to know God helped me to become more sensitive to people's needs and feelings."

"That's all well and good, but I can't let you put yourself in danger on my behalf."

She patted his hand. "Don't worry, I'm well protected."

His turn to roll eyes. "Another Christian thing, right?"

She smiled. "The 'whole armor of God.' Ephesians, Chapter Six, verses eleven through eighteen. You should read it sometime."

Returning her smile, he shook his head. "Maybe I will." He straightened in the chair. "Okay, we'll see how things go, but the minute things get heavy, you're out. Is that clear?"

"We'll see."

He threw up his hands in defeat. "You're crazy, you know that?"

"So I've been told," she said, winking.

Slade leaned toward her, took her hand. "In all seriousness, Stasi, it *is* nice to have someone there for me. You and Arlene are the only two people I can be absolutely sure of."

She cocked her head. "Speaking of which, that's another thing I've been thinking about lately." She knew she needed to tread carefully, not wanting to hinder any progress in their friendship. And somehow, she sensed that this was a delicate subject with Slade.

"Don't you have any family you could call? Someone close to you, perhaps, who may want to know how you are?"

"No." It came too quickly, and she knew that she had hit a nerve.

Taking his face between her hands, Stasi forced him to look deeply into her eyes. "Slade, you know I've always been honest with you. I think I deserve the same courtesy."

Looking away, he leaned back against the chair and emitted a heavy sigh.

Silence.

She thought he'd decided not to answer, but then he turned a soulful gaze on her and spoke quietly. "I have a mother. She lives in a condo I bought for her down in Florida."

"You haven't told her, have you?"

He stared down at his lap. "No. And I'm not going to."

"Slade, she has a right to know."

"I don't want her to worry. She's had enough of that to last a lifetime."

She stared at him, incredulous. "You're her son. She'd want to be with you."

"Which is another reason I don't want her to know. She'd hop on a plane and come up here, getting herself all involved, like you. If there *is* any danger, I don't want her here."

Stasi sighed in defeat. He was wrong. He was also right. A mother would want to be with her son at a time like this. But Slade's protectiveness was understandable. She only hoped that one day she would find out why it was so fierce.

He had been spending a lot of time watching Slade's apartment building from the parking lot on the other side of Chestnut Street. Day and night. Like a stakeout. What a laugh! He had no idea what he was doing. He was a brilliant executive. He did not have the mind of a criminal.

Scratch that.

Okay, he was a criminal. But not your typical stereotype. There was no stealing, drug dealing, killing . . .

Uh-oh. That was two out of three.

Scrubbing his hands over his face, he felt shame. He was sorry he'd ever gotten himself mixed up in this. His career was in jeopardy, he had compromised his morals, and he was about to lose a good friend.

Slade.

No! He wouldn't think about it. Anyhow, he'd do anything to keep himself out of jail.

He couldn't get into that building without its being known. Security was tight. Maybe if he goes out . . .

He looked down at the gun lying on the passenger seat. It was the only way. The thing was, he'd have to get pretty close. He'd never handled a gun before, so he was not a marksman.

Sinking low in the seat, he rested his head back. It might be a long wait.

CHAPTER TWENTY-FOUR

AFTER SHE SAW THAT SLADE WAS COMFORTABLY PLANTED in the passenger seat, Stasi settled herself behind the steering wheel.

"Are you sure it's safe to go now? We could wait another hour."

Slade pushed the tiny button on his watch to illuminate the face. "No, it'll be fine. Everyone's usually gone by nine."

"It's your use of the word *usually* that worries me," she replied, buckling her seatbelt.

Slade shrugged. "Even if we were caught, I have every right to be there."

She backed the car out of its slot. "But not if you're caught in someone else's office."

It was nine o'clock and he was just about ready to call it a night when he noticed two figures in the vestibule of Slade's apartment building. Snatching up the binoculars he'd been using, he focused in on the entrance and watched as the dark-haired beauty he remembered from Slade's party held the door while Slade wheeled through.

Well, *that* was interesting. He'd run into Melissa recently, so he knew she and Slade weren't an item anymore. In fact, he'd been contemplating asking her out himself. But Slade couldn't be hurting all that much if he'd hooked himself up with that she-cat.

They'd gotten into a car and pulled out of the parking lot, so he started his car and followed them from a safe distance. He'd stick it out and see what came of it. Maybe he'd find the opportunity to finish the job this time.

The night was clear but cool, and he found he needed to use the heater. Switching on the radio, he relaxed back against the seat. He figured that they'd be driving for a while, since they'd just left Haddonfield. But he was astonished when, only twenty minutes later, they turned onto Main Street.

"Take my flashlight so you don't have to turn on the overhead lights," Stasi told Slade after cutting the engine. "It's in the glove compartment."

Slade emitted a short laugh. "This isn't a spy movie, Stasi. The office lights will be fine."

"I guess I am getting a little carried away," she sighed. She got out of the car and went around to the trunk to retrieve Slade's wheelchair. When she brought it around, Slade was ready and deftly hoisted himself into it.

"You stay in the car. I'll make it as quick as I can." He began wheeling toward the entrance of the building.

"Wait!" Stasi slammed the car door and caught up. "Wouldn't it be quicker and easier if we both looked?"

He stopped rolling. Did she have to be so gung-ho? Even though he'd agreed to let her help, he wanted to keep her out of it as much as possible. "Look, it's safer in the car. Besides, I need you for a lookout in case anyone happens by."

She looked skeptically down at him and frowned. "Okay, you win. This time."

Slade flashed her a smile. "Thatagirl." Then he wheeled off, hoping that would appease her for a while. If she thought she was doing something important, it would be easier to keep her out of harm's way.

"How will I let you know if someone comes?" she called after him.

He spun the chair around and thought for a moment. "Let's see." An idea sprang into his head. "You have your cell phone with you?"

"Uh-huh," she said, nodding her head.

"Good. Ring the front desk twice, hang up, then ring once."

"Got it."

Something's up. Why else would they be going to the office like two thieves in the night?

He drove right on by when they turned onto Main Street, making a U-turn farther up, then doubling back.

Main Street was not your average, everyday avenue. It was more like a prestigious commercial district, surrounded by an iron gate with colorful flags hailing its entrance. It was also an elite residential area, with elegant condominiums situated to the far left of the business section.

Passing through the gates, he extinguished the headlights and slowly cruised toward the building. It was generally quiet this time of evening. Only a few of the businesses operated late into the night: a few restaurants, a banquet room. But none of those were located near Conrad, Mitchell's offices. He felt quite safe in doing what he needed to do.

Knowing Slade would recognize his car, he steered it around the back of the building. Peering through the windshield up toward the third-floor windows, he could see the office lights on. Reaching for the gun he'd left lying on the passenger seat, he swung out of the car.

"You're about to get the surprise of your life, Slade old buddy," he muttered under his breath.

CHAPTER TWENTY-FIVE

CROUCHING IN THE SEAT BEHIND THE WHEEL, STASI positioned herself so that she had A clear view of the window to Slade's office on the third floor. The building loomed over the car like a phantom, creating a dimness far deeper than surrounding areas of the parking lot.

Cell phone clasped tightly in one hand, she stared up at the lighted window expectantly. *What* she expected, she didn't know.

This was creepy. *Hurry, Slade*! It seemed he'd been in there for hours when in reality it had been only minutes.

As she peered up at the building, she caught a flutter of movement in her peripheral vision. Moving her head only slightly, she narrowed her eyes, straining to make out the shadowy figure skulking along the front of the building. Instantly her heart, her pulse, and her mind were racing.

On the cell phone, Stasi punched in Slade's office number with rapid precision. It rang once.

The figure—she assumed it was a man—was at the door. It looked as though he were using a key.

The second ring. She cut it off, punched in the number again.

He was inside now.

Ring! She cut it again and flung the phone down on the seat. Glancing up at the window, her breath caught in her throat when she saw the light go out.

What should she do? Did the intruder turn out the light, leaving Slade alone and defenseless in the dark? Could Slade have done it after she signaled him?

She couldn't just sit there and do nothing. Fumbling in the glove compartment, she snatched the flashlight and tore out of the car.

The phone was ringing. Once. Twice. It stopped. Slade stopped searching the desk and waited, his raspy breathing slicing through the silence. After an abbreviated pause, the phone rang again. Once.

Stasi's signal! He never thought she'd really need to use it. He'd devised that plan so she'd think she had something important to do and agree to stay in the car and out of danger.

But this meant that someone was coming, and he had to think fast. He wheeled over to the light switch, surprising himself at the speed with which he achieved it. Flicking off the light and leaving the door ajar, he rolled his chair backward, nudging into a tall file cabinet. Wheeling around it, he settled into the obscure, inky black corner it provided. Holding his breath, he waited.

The elevator dinged as it stopped on the third floor. After a few seconds, Slade heard a rattling sound, the sound of a key being used to unlock a door. Next, he heard a soft moaning sound. The reception area door; it emitted a heartrending groan of protest each time it was used. This one was long and drawn out, which meant that someone was trying to be inconspicuous and was failing miserably. Whoever it was caught on, because then Slade heard a short, sharp squeak and a soft, muted thud. He knew that the intruder had swung the door swiftly back in place, stopped just short of the frame, held the knob so that the tongue wouldn't click into place, then gently turned the knob back.

Now he understood how a blind person felt. He couldn't see, but all his other senses were humming with life. Just by the sounds, he had a clear, vivid picture of what was happening.

First there was nothing, then the whisper of shoe soles touching down on the soft carpet and coming closer.

He gripped the wheels of the chair with sweaty palms. Moist droplets broke out on his forehead and upper lip.

From his vantage point, Slade watched as a murky figure moved into the darkened room. He heard heavy breathing, smelled a musky cologne that seemed vaguely familiar but that he couldn't pinpoint.

Apparently, this person couldn't find a flashlight, or he chose not to use one for the sake of anonymity.

What should he do? How could he get out without being seen?

He didn't need to decide that for the moment. The black, velvety form pivoted and moved out of the room, leaving him a few precious seconds to devise a plan of action.

Upon opening the squealing door to the reception area, he discovered that the office was pitch black.

Great. He hadn't thought to bring a flashlight. Slithering around in the dark wasn't his bag, and he hadn't thought it would be Slade's.

If he turned on the light, he would be revealed in all his glory, and he didn't want that. Killing Slade was one thing. He had no other alternative. But he knew he wouldn't be able to stand the look that would be in Slade's eyes if he showed himself seconds before pulling the trigger.

He pushed the door closed—fast this time—stopping just short of the catch, before easing it into place. He cringed at the short, loud screech it made. Man! He'd have to have that taken care of.

While waiting for his eyes to adjust to the darkness, he decided it would be best to start with the office directly across from where he stood. He could handle that in the dark.

Still holding the gun in one hand, he moved across the room as lightly as he could, thrusting his arms out in front of him, as if some obstacle might jump into his path.

The door came against his hand and swung back as he pressed on into the center of the room. Not knowing what to do next, he stood there for a moment. It was too dark to see anything. Too dark to *do* anything. If he encountered Slade and the girl, what could he do in the dark? Thankfully, he'd had the foresight to leave the building door unlocked should the need arise for a quick getaway.

He then left the office, heading toward the other end of the hall.

Stasi found the stairs in the lobby and ran up with swift, short leaps. Good thing she wore jeans and sneakers. And good thing the stairs and halls were lit.

At the third floor, she pulled open the door to the hallway, hoping it wouldn't make too much noise. Relief washed over her when she felt the heavy pull of hydraulic pressure. Gently guiding the door closed, she turned and skimmed down the hall to Slade's office.

She was dismayed to find the door to Conrad, Mitchell closed. Trying the knob, she found that it turned, and she slowly pushed open the door.

Squeeeak!

Oh, no! She was sure that that could be heard from any of the offices within. Leaving the door open, she slipped in and crouched behind the receptionist's desk, not knowing what she'd do if she were found.

But she had to help Slade. Was he already lying injured somewhere close by? No. She wouldn't think that. Not after everything he'd already been through. She prayed for wisdom and guidance.

Slade heard the door again. Was the intruder leaving? He hadn't heard the door close. Then a thought rushed at him so swiftly it knocked him back. She wouldn't . . . Stasi!

He was ready to roll out of hiding when he heard feet thumping. Too late. The thumping came closer, then into the room. He waited. The shadowy form. It was too big to be Stasi.

Holding his breath, he watched the figure move toward his corner. Weak light filtered in from the open door to the hallway out front. Slade leaned into the side of the file cabinet, cupping his fingers along the corner edges. The silhouette came up even with the front of the cabinet. *Now!* Unsure of his muted tactility but with every ounce of strength he could muster, Slade propelled the monstrosity sideways. Drawers jutting forward, the cabinet tilted toward Slade's astonished would-be attacker. The man's scream was cut off by a sharp, loud crack before the unit overtook him on its way to the floor.

The now empty space where the cabinet had been provided enough room for Slade's wheelchair to pass. He sped through the door to the outer office. "Stasi!" he called in a stage whisper.

She sprang from behind the receptionist's desk. "Slade! What happened?"

"I'll explain later! Let's get out of here!"

Stasi ran into the hall while Slade followed in his wheelchair. Stopping at the elevator, she frantically pushed the "down" button. "Oh, Slade, he'll be out here before the elevator comes!"

"You take the stairs, it'll be quicker for you. I'll wait for the elevator."

"No! I won't leave you!" she cried, peering down the hallway, trembling.

"Go on! I won't have you hurt! Now go!"

"No!"

Just then, the elevator dinged and the doors slid open. Stasi thrust the flashlight she'd been holding onto Slade's lap, pushed him in, and punched the button.

Once in the lobby, she rushed Slade and herself through the doors and into the parking lot.

"It's going to take forever to get me into that car," Slade said as they raced toward it.

"Don't worry about it. Let's just do it!"

Swinging open the door, she positioned Slade. He was barely out of the chair before she had it folded up and deposited in the trunk, along with the flashlight.

"I'm impressed. That was really quick," he told her when she jumped in behind the wheel.

She jabbed her key into the ignition and started the engine. "I've done it so many times, I've got it down to a science."

"You're pretty handy to have around in an emergency." He grinned at her as they sped away from the building.

Eyes intent on the road, she shook her head at his remark.

"What's the matter?"

"Of all the qualities a girl wants to impress a guy with, I assure you, being handy is not one of them."

Inside the building, Troy Kent worked himself out from under the filing cabinet. How could he be so stupid? Apparently Slade Mitchell was not as helpless as he had thought. He'd be more careful next time. And more prepared.

They were getting away. Let them. Next time, he'd make sure there was no way out.

CHAPTER TWENTY-SIX

IN THE CAR ON THE WAY HOME, SLADE TOLD STASI exactly what happened at the office. One thing worried him, however. "I'm reasonably sure that as the guy went down with the cabinet, I heard a gunshot."

"Yes, now that you mention it, I remember hearing something that could have been that, but it didn't register at the time. It was hard to tell, considering all the chaos." She paused. "You know, you were great, back there. I was so wo. . ." She caught herself, realizing that what she almost said would injure his ego.

Slade impaled her with a knowing glare. "What were you going to say, Stasi?"

"Nothing," she answered, her eyes fixed on the road.

"You were worried I wouldn't be able to take care of myself, weren't you?"

She didn't answer.

"C'mon, Stasi. It was you who reminded me earlier about honesty. Don't I deserve the courtesy now?"

Ashamed, she glanced at him nervously. "Okay, you're right. I was worried." When he didn't respond, she glanced again, but she couldn't read his face, as it was turned toward the window. "Are you mad?"

"No," he answered in a quiet voice. "I don't blame you. I wasn't so sure myself."

"Well, you proved us both wrong," she said matter-of-factly. "But I gotta tell you, my imagination ran rampant at the thought that you could have been killed."

He turned in the darkness of the car, piercing her with a fierce gaze. "Maybe you, too," he pointed out.

She hadn't thought of that. She had been thinking only of *him* the whole time. Stunned by his words, she stole a glance at him. "Y-you could be right. But that doesn't. . ."

"No buts, Stasi," he interrupted. "We agreed that if it got dangerous for you, you'd stay out of it."

"No, *you* agreed. I won't leave you to do this on your own. You're stuck with me now."

"C'mon, Stasi! Stop acting like a horse's. . ." he broke off abruptly, ". . .hindquarters," he finished, lamely.

Appreciating that he respected her enough to curb his profanity for her, she glanced at him indignantly. "I beg your pardon, but I'm not the one acting like a horse's hindquarters, you are! I'm *in*, and that's that."

"Why?" he asked, sounding incredulous. "*Why* would you do this for me?"

She continued driving in silence. She didn't have an answer.

Once home, Slade put in a call to Detective Jessup and had to wait for his return call. When it came, he relayed the events of the evening, including his suspicion of the gunshot.

"We'll check it out in the morning, Mr. Mitchell. You understand, though, that everything will be brought out into the open."

"I understand, Detective. At least I know the truth. Somebody *is* trying to kill me."

Later, Stasi lay in her bed, unable to sleep. Never mind that Slade could have been killed tonight. Or that it was someone he knew and was probably close to. Or even that she could have been killed herself. The thing that was keeping her awake was that question Slade had asked her on the way home.

Why *was* she getting herself involved in this whole mess? Was it *just* because it was the Christian thing to do? Or was there more to it than that?

She turned on her side, disgusted with herself. Deep down, she knew the answer. There *was* more to it. But she was afraid to admit what "more" it could be.

She couldn't let it be more. Even though Slade's lifestyle had changed since the accident, he was still an unbeliever. There was no future for them. Any romantic relationship they might foster had a huge strike against it already, for doesn't Scripture say that we should not be unequally yoked?

Furthermore, she doubted that Slade had the same inclinations toward her. He was undoubtedly in a state of emotional turmoil, what with the knowledge that he's a target for murder, his physical loss, his breakup with Melissa.

Restless, she twisted onto her other side. Then, of course, there was that old hurt embedded deep into the chambers of her heart. Could she afford to free those feelings she had buried for so long? She wasn't sure she could risk it, in light of Slade's situation. Hadn't she done it before, only to be crushed when she'd lost Barry? No, she couldn't handle it again. Of course, the anguish of her belief that Barry's death was mostly her fault made it doubly hard to accept.

Flopping onto her back, she knew she needed to pray, so she did—for the Lord to take away the burden of her guilt about Barry, for Slade's situation, for wisdom in their relationship, whatever it may be, and for God's will through it all.

With the assistance of the Voorhees Police Department, Jessup and Burns obtained a search warrant and arrived at the offices of Conrad, Mitchell, Kent, and Schriver, along with two local uniformed police officers, on Wednesday morning after taking statements from Slade and Stasi.

Upon investigating the office where the alleged incident had taken place, they found, standing to the left of the door, a tall, beige, metal file cabinet that was dented and slightly misshapen, its drawers not fitting flush. A thorough perusal of the room turned up a bullet lodged in the snow-white ceiling. One of the uniformed officers removed it with a tweezers and dropped it into a plastic bag.

The office belonged to Clark Schriver, but that didn't mean that Mr. Schriver was the perpetrator. Jessup had just opened his mouth to question Clark, when Troy Kent swept into the room.

Troy's features registered surprise for a brief second at the sight of Jessup and Burns, then transformed into a blank expression as he immediately excused himself, retreating hastily down the hall to his office.

Neither Jessup nor Burns missed the reddish-purple bruise extending beyond the edges of a large adhesive bandage on the left side of Troy's forehead.

"Mr. Kent!" Jessup called as he and Frank followed Troy down the hall. Troy didn't answer and kept walking. "Mr. Kent!" Jessup said again as Troy disappeared through the door to his office and slammed it shut.

Jessup knocked, then pushed through the door, Burns on his heels.

Troy stood up from where he was sitting behind his desk.

"Mr. Kent," Jessup began, "we have a search warrant, and we'd like to start with your office."

Troy's handsome face went white. "Of course." He moved out from behind the desk and stood by the door.

Detective Jessup was impressed with the desk. It was huge, shiny, solid oak. Neat as a pin. He began searching the drawers, but it didn't take long. Reaching all the way to the back of the top drawer, he pulled out a .38 revolver. Examining it, he could tell that it had recently been fired, and he would bet that the bullet taken from the ceiling would match it.

"Are you licensed to have this gun in your possession, Mr. Kent?" Jessup asked Troy.

By this time, the other officers had entered the room and some employees were gathered at the door. Troy's eyes bulged while droplets appeared on his forehead and above his lip. "I . . . no, I don't."

"We're placing you under arrest, Mr. Kent," Jessup told him as one of the uniformed officers stepped forward, brandishing a pair of handcuffs.

CHAPTER TWENTY-SEVEN

LATE WEDNESDAY AFTERNOON, SLADE WHEELED THROUGH
Stasi's doorway. Recently they had taken to leaving the doors to
both apartments wide open, drifting between the two, dispens-
ing with the formality of knocking.

Stasi, at the kitchen counter preparing a fresh pot of coffee,
stopped and watched Slade approach. His face was twisted in
anxiety.

"I just spoke with Detective Jessup. You're never going to
believe this—I don't believe it myself—but they've arrested
Troy Kent." He rattled the words off so fast they all but tripped
over one another.

"Troy Kent?" The name was familiar, but she couldn't put
her finger on it.

"One of my business partners. One of my closest friends."
Obviously seeing her puzzlement, he added, "Remember that
jerk who hit on you at my party?"

Recognition registered. "Oh," she nodded. "Yes, I remember." Her eyes grew as round as golf balls. "You mean *he* was the one . . .?"

Slade nodded. "Yep, he was the one." Propping his elbows on the armrests of the wheelchair, he leaned his forehead on his palms. "I can't believe it. We were so close. How could he have deceived me so easily?"

"Come into the living room, Slade." She moved toward the sofa, and he followed, parking the wheelchair before it. However, as Stasi turned to sit, she was taken aback by Slade's sudden action. All at once, his arms were wrapped around her waist, his face buried against her tailored shirt.

She could understand. It must hurt to know that someone you were so fond of, whom you trusted at every turn, was the one who hated you enough to want to kill you.

Stroking his hair, she remained there, hoping to sustain him, wishing that her strength, her faith, would seep from her pores and into his being, to wash away the sea of pain in which he was drowning.

Finally, she gently pulled away from him and sat before him on the sofa. Taking his hands, she said, "Listen to me. I can imagine how you feel, how you must be hurting. The only thing you can do now is give it to God and move on."

He hung his head. "It's not that easy."

"I know. We tend to hang on to things. Try to make them right on our own."

Puffing out a weary sigh, he said, "Stasi, please. I'm not in the mood for one of your religious lectures right now."

She released his hands, bowed her head to study her own, which she had placed on her lap.

"I need to be alone, right now. I'm going back to my apartment." He paused without moving. "You understand, don't you?"

She only nodded in answer.

Her head snapped up at the thud of his door across the hall closing and the click of the deadbolt being driven home.

The mere thought of Slade shutting her out was not the only thing that left her unsettled. A fleeting second during the course of their conversation had struck her, but it had faded away with her concern for Slade's apparent anguish over his friend. She sat for some time, sipping coffee and going over and over it. What *was* it? Slade had come in upset. He told her his friend was arrested. She didn't quite recognize the name until—*that's it*! She couldn't wait to tell Slade. He hadn't even noticed, himself. This would lift his spirits!

But then, she knew she had to wait. He obviously needed to be alone for a while, to work through the tangle of feelings wreaking havoc with his emotions.

She would practically burst, but she would wait.

Troy sat alone in his darkened living room. He hadn't moved from the corner of the sofa since he had arrived home earlier that day. It was dusk, but he hadn't bothered to turn on a lamp.

He kept replaying the events of the past two days in his mind. He had been searched, arrested, and charged with several violations, ranging from illegal possession of a weapon to murderous intent.

At the police station, they had taken his personal effects and had taken mug shots and fingerprints. The humiliation of posing for those pictures remained with him even now, and his fingers still bore traces of the black ink they'd been pressed into. Even more than all that, he still shivered at the horror of being transported to the county jail in Camden.

The county jail. That was the worst nightmare of all, and he never wanted to go through it again. He had been treated like a common criminal. Once strip-searched and forced to relinquish his stylish clothes for an orange prison jumpsuit, he had been put into an overcrowded jail cell with what he perceived as hardened criminals.

They reeked. So did the cell. And the bedding, if you could call it that. And the one filthy toilet shared by three other men he didn't even know—didn't want to know.

Fortunately, the men had left him to himself, except to call him "Pretty Boy." Perhaps it was because he made no effort to speak with them in any way. But being locked up with two hulking black men and one smart-alecky Hispanic was so overwhelming that he just sat on his bunk, pressing himself so hard against the cinder-block wall, he thought he'd become a part of it. And he'd slept in that same position all night.

Sheriff's officers had taken him, handcuffed and shackled across the street to the Hall of Justice for his preliminary hearing Thursday morning. There in the courtroom were John Conrad and the attorney John had promised to retain for Troy when he was arrested the previous day.

Based on a sparkling clean record thus far and the fact that the prosecutor's case was "a little weak," Troy had been released on bail, which John had posted.

John again. He'd been so good to Troy through all of this. If it hadn't been for John, he wouldn't be sitting in his own living room right this minute. He must never let him down again.

He had been home since midafternoon. Contemplating. He had wanted to return the gun to its rightful owner, but he should never have taken it to the office. BIG MISTAKE! What would happen to him now? Would he be sentenced to prison for years and years? He shook his head. No. He couldn't take that after last night's experience. He'd rather die.

Suddenly, it all became very clear to him. He pushed off the sofa, went to his desk across the room, and switched on the lamp. Pulling open the top drawer, he retrieved a legal pad and pen, sat down, and began writing.

CHAPTER TWENTY-EIGHT

THERE WAS A LIGHT RAP ON THE DOOR. "SLADE? IT'S ME," came the soft, honey-sweet voice he'd become accustomed to hearing through all of his waking hours.

"Ninety-eight, ninety-nine, one hundred." He lowered the weights he'd been one-arm lifting to the floor and dabbed at his face with the towel he had draped around his neck.

"Slade?" Stasi called through the door. "Can I come in?"

His waking hours were not the only time he heard that voice, he thought, as he rolled his chair out through the living room and toward the door. Lately, it had been invading his dreams, too. He halted at the door and paused.

Invade.

Yes, that was the word for it. It was not only her voice, but also her presence—even her nonpresence. She always seemed to be here in this apartment with him, even when she wasn't.

It was an invasion, all right. Of his time, his privacy, his . . . senses.

He wasn't going there now.

"Slade!" She sounded angry now. "I know you're in there. You can't hide forever."

He wasn't really hiding. Or was he? Maybe he was, but she couldn't guess what from, and he wasn't even sure himself.

Sliding back the bolt, he opened the door and wheeled aside to allow her entrance. She stormed past him. By the time he'd closed the door and turned the wheelchair around, her anger had dissipated.

"How are you?" she asked, her eyes soft.

"Fine."

"What have you been up to?"

"Working out."

"Stupid question. I guess I should have known," she added, making a motion with her hand to indicate his appearance. "Do you need anything? You look beat."

"No, I'm fine." He rolled himself into his combination office and exercise room, lifted the hand weights, and began pumping iron with the ferocity of an angry lion.

Stasi leaned against the edge of the computer center. "Have you eaten? I have some leftover casserole I could heat up in a jiff."

"No. Not hungry," he forced out between lifts.

She expelled a frustrated puff of breath. "How long have you been at this?"

"Don't know. Four or five hours," still pumping.

"Slade, why are you doing this to yourself?"

He stopped lifting and wiped his face with the towel again. "Doing what?" he asked remotely.

"Punishing yourself."

He looked up at her. "I'm not punishing myself. I just need to work through some things, and this is the only way I know how."

Just then the phone on the desk jangled, nearly sending Stasi across the room in one leap. Slade didn't move. It rang again. Since he still hadn't made any move to answer it, Stasi turned to reach for it.

"No!" he boomed, causing her to snatch her hand back as if it had been burned. "Leave it. The machine will pick it up."

Two more rings, a click, then his own voice, sounding sunny and cheerful, rang out from the recorded greeting. The way he used to sound and hadn't sounded since before the accident. Then reality hit like a swift punch to the stomach. This *was* him before the accident. Whatever happened to that happy-go-lucky guy? He had to be in there somewhere.

A shrill voice cut into his cogitation. A familiar woman's voice, leaving a message.

"Slade? It's Mom. Are you there? Where have you been? You never return my calls. This isn't like you. We haven't spoken for months! I need to know if you're okay. If you don't call me soon, I'm going to get on a plane and come up there!" Click.

All through the message, Stasi eyed him pleadingly to pick up while he shook his head and shot her a mind-your-own-business look.

"You're awful," she said when the message ended.

"You're just finding that out?"

"Hmph!"

"Look, I'm just not ready to let her see me like this."

"You heard her, she's coming soon anyway."

"I'll deal with it when the time comes."

"But how have you avoided her for so long? Hasn't she called your office? Someone there could tell her."

"The day I came out of the coma, I thought of her. I knew she'd call the office if she couldn't reach me at home. I left strict instructions that the receptionist was to take messages on all personal calls, then give them to Arlene to give to me. I also told them that under no circumstances was anyone to tell a caller of my situation."

"What about all that time you were in the coma? Didn't anyone try to contact her?"

"No one at the office would be able to. I never saw a need to give any of them her address or phone number. Not even Arlene."

Her heart aching for this woman, she shook her head.

Brring!

For the second time in just a few minutes, Slade saw Stasi almost jump out of her skin. "I think you should find some other place to stand."

After Slade's greeting, a man's hesitant, slightly slurred voice came on. "Slade? It's Troy."

Slade wildly motioned for Stasi to pick up for him, which she did and practically tossed the receiver at him.

"I guess you don't want. . ."

Troy was cut off by Slade's answer. "Troy?"

"Slade. I didn't think you'd feel like talking to me."

He didn't know how he felt. On the one hand, he was devastated. Yet at the same time, it was strangely comforting to know your would-be killer was someone you had been close to for a long time. "Go on," was all he said.

"I . . . I just want to say how sorry I am. I didn't really *want* to do it, but when you started asking questions about Mrs. Haloran, I felt I had no choice."

"You had a choice, Troy. You could have come to me. Whatever the problem was, we could have worked it out together."

Troy's anguished sigh rushed through the receiver. "Not this, buddy. There was no way to work this out. What's done is done. I tried twice and failed."

There was a pause, and Slade heard the swish of liquid and a gulp. "Are you drinking, Troy?"

"Yeah. Remember how you and I used to do the club scene? Those were the days." Slade heard him take another swig. "Anyhow, I have to dull the senses in preparation for what happens next."

"What do you mean?"

"Never mind. Listen, I wrote out a confession that will explain everything."

Slade didn't like where this seemed to be heading. "Why write it? Just enter a guilty plea at your trial."

"Good-bye, friend. Have a good life."

Something in the sound of Troy's voice triggered an alarm in Slade's head. There was a finality to it. "Troy, wait!" Stasi looked at him, her eyes full of concern.

"Just always remember how sorry I am, Slade," Troy mumbled. "Wait!" Slade yelled again as he heard a brief rattling sound, then a soft thud, as if Troy had tried unsuccessfully to replace the receiver and it had fallen to the floor. The alcohol must have done its job. Then, listening intently, and from a distance, he heard a metallic click. "Troy, what . . . Have you gotten another gun?" Immediately after, the sound of gunshot exploded into his ear and reverberated through his head. His upper body snapped back as if he, himself, had been hit with the force of a bullet, causing him to drop the phone.

Stasi was instantly at his side. "Slade! What happened?"

For a second, Slade just sat there, trembling and staring at the phone on the floor. In the next instant, he came alive. "Go get my cell phone on the table in the living room and call the Voorhees police. Hurry!

After Stasi rushed off, Slade bent over and, hands shaking, fumbled for the phone on the floor. "Troy!" he yelled into the receiver. "C'mon, Troy, don't do this!" He didn't really expect an answer, knowing it was already too late.

CHAPTER TWENTY-NINE

TRUE TO HIS WORD, TROY EXPLAINED EVERYTHING IN HIS written confession. After Stasi called the police, Slade asked her to notify Detective Jessup of what had happened. A copy of the confession was faxed to Jessup and Burns, who in turn took a copy over for Slade to read.

Troy confessed to embezzling funds from vulnerable citizens and investing them in phony companies. When he found out that Slade was asking questions, he knew Slade wouldn't rest until he had uncovered the whole operation and would want to do the honest and legitimate thing. Not relishing the idea of a prison term, he had rigged Slade's parachute to look like he'd been killed in a freak accident. When that failed, he had watched and followed Slade, finally ending with the encounter at the office on Tuesday night. After spending just one night in jail, he knew he could never spend *years* in one, so he had decided that he was better off dead.

"Well, Mr. Mitchell," Detective Jessup had said to Slade before leaving, "looks like this case is wrapped up. You can rest easy now."

When Stasi had closed the door after the two detectives, Slade shook his head and said, "Rest easy? Easy for him to say. This whole nightmare has left my life in a shambles. Nothing will ever be the same again."

Not knowing what to say to that, Stasi went to the refrigerator and retrieved two small bottles of water. She could understand how he felt, but she also knew he needed to move on. "Let's just thank the Lord that you still have your life." She uncapped one of the bottles and handed it to Slade.

"Hah! You really think I should thank God for *this*?" he asked, moving his free hand up and down the length of his body and indicating its present condition.

"Think about it," she said, uncapping the second bottle of water. After drinking deeply, she added, "You still have *your* life. Troy doesn't."

Appearing not to have heard her, Slade absently took a swig from the bottle and stared at the floor. His eyes were unfocused, as if watching a scene being played out in another time and place. "Now that I think about it, Troy had plenty of time to rig my chute that day. He must have done it under the guise of loading my stuff into his trunk. Said he had to move things around to make room for it."

Quietly lowering herself onto the sofa, Stasi realized that this was another returning memory. Slade wasn't even aware of it. She knew he needed time to work through this, but it seemed he hardly had time to work through everything else that had happened. Poor Slade. Things just kept piling up. Could this be the right time to tell him what she had come earlier to tell him? It was worth a shot if it let even a small ray of light through these dark days that he had lately been experiencing.

She cleared her throat. "Slade, when I arrived earlier today, it was because I had something important to tell you."

"Yes?" he asked, still staring at the floor.

She set her water bottle down on the end table next to her. "Remember when you came to my apartment to tell me about Troy?"

He nodded, still not looking at her.

"Well, you said something that I didn't catch at first, but then I realized what it was. Only *you* didn't catch it either."

He looked up at her now. "Well, what *is* it, Stasi?" he asked, sounding frustrated with her rambling.

"When I didn't recognize Troy's name, you asked me if I remembered the jerk who hit on me at your party."

"So?"

"*Slade*," she said, widening her eyes and shooting him a meaningful look. "That party took place shortly before the skydiving accident. It occurred during the period of time affected by your memory loss!"

A myriad of emotions paraded across Slade's handsome features. Puzzlement, shock, and finally, elation. "You're right, Stasi! I never even realized it! My memory must be returning!"

"Yes! And you did the same thing a moment ago when you remembered Troy putting your gear in his trunk!"

All at once, they were laughing and crying together. Stasi took Slade's water bottle from him, placed it on the table beside hers, then flung herself onto his lap, hugging him while Slade twirled the wheelchair around in circles, and even popped wheelies.

When the laughter died away and all was still, Stasi found herself staring deeply down into Slade's dark eyes, her arms circling his neck. His face was so close she felt the tickle of his breath on her cheek as it ruffled the delicate wisp of hair that had clung to it. In her peripheral vision, she saw Slade release the wheels of the chair and place his hands on her arms. Slowly, he slid them up to her shoulders, then farther up to gently cradle her head between them. His eyes still held her captive, and her breath caught in her throat as he pulled her head even closer, enabling him to press his lips tenderly against hers.

The kiss was timid at first, but then it deepened while Stasi's heart did a joyous tap dance against her ribcage. But a small voice at the back of her mind was whispering that she should not be allowing this to happen.

Slade wrapped his arms around her, pulling her closer. Then he broke the kiss abruptly, pulling back as if he'd been burned. Grasping Stasi's shoulders and pushing her back, he stammered, "Stasi, I . . . get up!"

Shocked and embarrassed, she scrambled out of his lap, hopping to her feet. Not knowing what to say or do, she took the time to compose herself while pretending to finger-comb and smooth back her hair.

"Stasi, I . . . I don't know what to say," Slade said from behind her.

"You don't have to say anything." She told him over her shoulder.

"I'm sorry, I shouldn't have done it. I know how you feel. . ."

"No!" She whirled around. "*I'm* the one who should apologize, throwing myself at you like that. I'm ashamed of myself, Slade. I don't know how I could ever do such a thing. I-it isn't like me."

"You were just caught up in the moment, sharing in my joy. That wasn't a problem. In fact . . ."

"What?" she asked when he didn't finish.

"Never mind."

"Fine. It's getting late. I'd better go." She turned and started toward the door, but the sound of his voice stopped her midstride.

"Stasi."

"Yes?" she answered without turning around.

"Did you . . . Are you sorry I kissed you?"

Turning back to face him, she said, "You weren't the only one doing the kissing, you know. In case you hadn't noticed, I kissed you back."

One corner of his mouth lifted in a cocky grin. "I definitely noticed."

"Uuugh!" She turned toward the door again, yanked it open, and left the apartment. Before closing the door, she poked her head in. "By the way, in answer to your question . . . and this worries me: No, I'm not sorry we kissed!" After slamming the door, she scurried across to her own apartment, accompanied by the muffled sound of Slade's deep-throated laughter.

CHAPTER THIRTY

IT WAS FRIDAY NIGHT, AND STASI HAD BEEN INVITED TO Slade's apartment for dinner. And *he* was doing the cooking!

That morning as she sat working at her computer, he had rolled through her open door and announced that he would be cooking dinner for the two of them to celebrate his case being closed and his partial memory return and to show his appreciation for her help in every aspect of his present situation. She had been a little taken aback at his complete turnaround from the day before. But it was good to see him cheerful again.

Her main concern at the moment was what to wear this evening. She wanted to look nice after all the jeans, sweats, and sneakers Slade had seen her in lately.

For some reason, she felt that tonight was going to be special. Their relationship had reached a new level, and even though he hadn't mentioned it, she knew Slade felt the same way.

Now that the weather was turning chilly, she could wear something long and sweepy. Reaching into the closet, she pulled out an elegant, burgundy, long-sleeved, knit dress. The mid-length flared skirt swirled and glided around her slender form with every move, and the sweetheart-shaped yoke accentuated her delicate, swanlike neck.

Giving herself a nod of approval in the full-length mirror in her bedroom, she then expertly applied a light touch of mascara and blush, added a dab of colorless lip gloss, and topped it off with a pearl choker necklace to match the pearl studs in her ears. After sliding into a pair of simple black pumps, she picked up the bottle of ginger ale and the cake she had bought to take with her and made her way over to Slade's.

She knew she shouldn't be so excited about the evening, nor should she be starting something she knew she couldn't finish. Although Slade had changed in many ways, he was still an unbeliever. But there was a special bond between them now; especially after all they'd been through together. They had formed a special friendship, and she couldn't just throw that away. So just for a little while, she'd allow herself this luxury.

The door to his apartment was closed, so, apprehensive about just walking in, she rang the doorbell. After a minute, Slade pulled the door open, and Stasi was rewarded with the gleam of admiration reflected in his eyes.

"Wow," he said, looking her over appreciatively. "Come on in." He whirled his chair around and rolled into the living room. As she followed, a whiff of his cologne wafted back toward her.

Apparently, Slade also felt this was a special occasion. He wore black dress slacks, a mauve dress shirt, and gray wool sport coat, no tie.

"Ditto," Stasi remarked belatedly.

"What?" He stole a glance at her over his shoulder.

"You look pretty good, too."

"Oh. Thanks."

From the living room, she could see into the dining area. She pulled in a breath, surprised at the array of china, silverware, and stemware Slade had used to set the table, complete with floral centerpiece and lit tapered candles.

"Slade, the table looks lovely."

"Thank you. I had a little help, though."

"Help?"

"Yes. I asked Arlene to pick up a few things for me."

"Oh," she said, still gazing in awe at the beautifully set table.

"She picked up the centerpiece, candles, and some groceries. I already had the china and utensils, and I *did* set the table myself."

Stasi felt a tingle run up her arms at the thought that he had done all of this with her in mind.

"Have a seat at the table and we'll get started."

She suddenly remembered the ginger ale and cake. "Oh, here. I brought these," she said, holding them up. "Where shall I put them?"

"Leave the bottle on the table and put the cake on the kitchen counter."

Stasi complied with the cake, but when she returned to the dining area to place the ginger ale on the table, she noticed that Slade already had a bottle of the same on ice. He had thought of everything.

She sniffed the air. "Mmm, something smells good. What are we having?" she asked, taking the seat Slade had pulled out for her.

Knowing he couldn't push it in under her, she performed the task herself.

"Shrimp cocktail as an appetizer, garden salad, and lemon pepper chicken. Dessert will be a surprise."

"Wow, I'm impressed."

"Don't be too impressed. To be honest, the salad is the pre-mixed kind, and the chicken is the type that's already prepared and all you have to do is pop it in the microwave. And, of course, the shrimp cocktail is easy. You buy the shrimp and the cocktail sauce, arrange them in a serving dish, and *voila*!

"There's nothing wrong with that," she replied as he wheeled into the kitchen. "You're a cook for the new millennium, but you still put it all together."

He wheeled out of the kitchen bearing a large bowl of salad on his lap. "I have to admit, I never *was* much of a cook, but I'm a whiz with a microwave," he said, flashing a grin and waggling his eyebrows.

Stasi laughed lightly at his quip, thinking that this was more like the old Slade.

He began dishing out the salad, and Stasi, not used to being waited on, felt useless. "Shall I pour the drinks?"

"No, you're not to move a muscle." He raised his chin and glared down his nose at her in a mock-haughty manner. "I will be at your complete disposal this evening to show my appreciation for all you've done for me these past months."

She laughed. "Oh, Slade, there's no need . . ."

He held up a hand, preventing her from going further. "I want to," he said, his face sincere.

Recognizing that this was also something he needed to do, she relented. "Okay, Slade. Slave away," she said, moving her arms in a flourishing gesture.

She watched him pour the ginger ale into her glass but was both touched and surprised that he honored her own Christian convictions by pouring the same into his own glass.

When he disappeared into the kitchen again, then returned with the shrimp cocktail, she clutched both sides of the seat of her chair in an effort to suppress a tremendous urge to spring up and help him perform this simple task. Slade carried a shrimp cocktail in each hand, thereby leaving no way to wheel his chair over to the table. He solved the dilemma by using his feet, taking small, painstaking steps to drag the wheelchair forward. Not only was this time-consuming, but she could see that it involved extreme effort and determination. Again, she was touched.

After arranging the shrimp cocktail at each place setting, Slade positioned himself at the head of the table, where a chair was conspicuously absent. Stasi was seated to his right, and he reached over and took her hand. "I know you always pray before a meal, so will you do the honors?" Without waiting for an answer, he bowed his head.

Stasi was so flabbergasted, she was unable to start right in, so she cleared her throat to give herself time to collect her thoughts. Finally, after a long moment, she was able to proceed.

"Father, we thank You for this bountiful meal, and for the hands that prepared it. We also thank You for Your grace and healing power, which enabled us to cultivate this beautiful friendship. In Your Son's name, we pray. Amen."

As they sat eating, they chatted happily about everything from the weather to the World Series, with Stasi interjecting remarks about the texture of the shrimp and the crispness of the salad.

When Slade served the main course, he carried it into the dining area in the same manner as the shrimp, except that an oven mitt protected each hand.

After the meal was over, they lingered over coffee and a cheesecake from MacMillan's Bakery, along with the cake that Stasi had brought. Sitting there, Stasi was suddenly overcome with a deep sense of tranquility and satisfaction. The meal was perfect and wonderful. The conversation was perfect and wonderful. In fact, the entire evening was perfect and wonderful! It had been a long time since she felt this way. She had to admit, Slade sure knew how to woo a girl.

Woo? Was Slade wooing her? It sure seemed like it, but . . . Perhaps he was just being nice, friendly. People do nice things for their friends, right?

She would not analyze it now, for tonight she was Cinderella, and she would just relax and savor the wonder of it.

The phone ringing jolted her from her languorous thoughts.

Slade looked at her pointedly and said, "Let's just enjoy the evening with no interruptions."

After the greeting, a familiar woman's voice crackled through the answering machine. "Slade? Are you there, son? Please pick up. I need to know if you're okay."

Stasi covered Slade's large hand with her own small one. "Please, Slade. You're putting her through torture."

His mother was leaving a lengthy message, and after a moment's thought, Slade said, "Okay, you're right." Wheeling himself over to the living room, he added, "You caught me in a good mood, you know," before picking up on the cordless phone. "Hello, Mom."

Stasi didn't want to be privy to this conversation taking place between mother and son for the first time in many months, but given the fact that Slade didn't take it in his office, she couldn't help it. She stayed at the table and scraped the remains of cheese-cake from her plate.

After a long silence, she heard Slade say, "Whoa, Mom! How can I answer any of your questions if you keep firing them at me with barely a breath in between?" A brief moment of silence, then, "Let me start at the beginning."

Stasi stood up and went to the kitchen to pour another cup of coffee, but she could still hear Slade's voice clearly.

"Yes, I'm still in a wheelchair and likely to be for the rest of my life. I may be able to walk some, but not all the time. Hardly ever, as a matter of fact," Slade was saying as she returned to the dining room and sat down at the table. Another pause. "Now, don't cry, Mom. Please?" There was an anxious tone to his voice. "*I'm* taking care of me. I've learned how. Besides, I have a wonderful friend who lives across the hall, and she's been a tremendous help." Pause. "Married? When did I say that?"

Stasi's head shot up at this. Slade sounded genuinely surprised himself. Had he planned on marrying Melissa before the accident? The thought caused a pang of jealousy to rip through her.

"That was probably before the accident. No, she's not the one. That would have been Melissa, but she's no longer in the picture." There was another brief pause while his mother spoke. "You're right. You have no idea how *many* things have changed since the accident. But it's times like this when you find out who *really* cares about you."

Stasi got up and began clearing the table. She hoped Slade had been talking about *her* in that last statement.

"Don't do that," Slade yelled over to her. "I told you I wanted to do *everything* tonight."

Shaking her head, she made a waving motion with her hand for him to return to the phone conversation, then continued carrying cups and plates to the kitchen.

"Yes, she's here. I cooked her dinner to show my appreciation for all she's done," she heard him say. "Yep. Yep. And she's beautiful, too, Mom." This made Stasi blush as she placed a cup into the dishwasher. Well, Slade certainly held nothing back from his mother. When he finally got talking to her, that is. She supposed that it had always been that way between them.

"Okay, she'd be delighted, I'm sure." Slade called Stasi into the living room, and when she approached wiping her hands on a towel, he held the phone out to her. "She wants to talk to you."

Her eyes widened. "Me?" she whispered. Slade nodded. "Why? What do I say?" Slade shrugged and jabbed the phone in her direction.

She dropped the dish towel onto a chair and took the phone in her shaky hand. What did Slade's mother want with her? "Hello?"

"Hello, this is Lois Mitchell, Slade's mother." She sounded as though she were still on the verge of tears.

"Hello. My name is Stasi Courtland."

"A very aristocratic name. Slade tells me you've been wonderful to him. You know, helping him after his accident and all."

"Yes, I live close by, and I'm pretty much available anytime he needs something."

"I'm so glad someone was there for him, since I couldn't be. Through no fault of my own, I might add. That was very inconsiderate of Slade to keep it from me."

"I agree. I've tried several times to make him return your calls."

"Okay, that's enough!" Slade cut in, making like he was trying to grab for the phone. I don't need the two of you ganging up on me."

"Thank you, dear. You seem like a girl after my own heart," Lois said.

"You're very welcome."

"It's been very nice to talk with you. Can you put Slade back on?"

"Sure. And it's been a pleasure talking with you, too." She handed the phone back to Slade.

"I'm back, Mom. No, it's not necessary for you to come right now. I'm fine. Tell you what, though. Why don't you come for the holidays? It's not that far off. You could come for Thanksgiving and leave after the New Year. Great. I know, I know. But I didn't want you to see me that way and worrying over me." A longer pause. "I know. You're right. I guess I should have told you sooner. I'm sorry, Mom. See you in November." He pushed the "end" button.

"I like your mom. She sounds sweet," Stasi told him as he replaced the phone in its base.

"Yeah, she is sweet. The greatest."

The pure adoration she saw reflected in Slade's eyes had Stasi hoping that she would inspire those emotions in any children she might one day have of her own.

Slade was quiet all of a sudden. He sat in the chair with his elbow propped on the arm and his mouth resting against his closed fist.

"What's wrong, Slade?"

His face registering incredibility, he blew out a puff of air. "Something my mother said just hit me."

"What was it?"

He looked up at her. "Shortly before the accident, I told my mother I was thinking of asking someone to marry me."

Stasi dropped into the chair where she left the dish towel. Was he thinking that he wanted to try again with Melissa? "Yes, I heard you say that."

He leaned closer to her. "Do you realize that if I hadn't had that accident . . . I should say, if Troy hadn't tried to kill me . . . I might have married Melissa before finding out how shallow she is?"

Stasi closed her eyes and sagged slightly in relief. The reason for this relief was something she wasn't ready to admit to herself.

"I guess you could say," he went on, "that in a roundabout way, that accident saved me from a fate worse than death," he finished wryly.

Stasi smiled, shaking her head. "It's great that you can think of it in those terms."

He turned and pinned her with an intense gaze. "There's something else I've been thinking about lately. I think you can guess what it is."

Stasi swallowed hard, but her eyes never left his. "Yes, I think I know what you're talking about."

He drew in a slow, deep breath, then let it out. "Stasi, that kiss the other day . . . I . . . I just don't know where any of this can go."

"I know. I feel the same way."

"I'm really in no shape to be involved with anyone and I don't know if I'll ever be."

Stasi nodded.

"I care for you a lot. I do, but . . ." She stopped him, placing two fingers against his lips.

"Listen, Slade," she said softly, "I care for you, too. But we both obviously have a lot of things to iron out before we can enter into a fully giving relationship with each other."

Her fingers were still pressed against his lips. He took her hand, kissing those fingers, before pulling her hand down and holding it in his own. "I know what *I* have to iron out, but just what is it exactly that *you* need to iron out?"

"Not so much ironing out, but just some things I need to heed as far as Scripture is concerned."

"What things?"

She pulled her hand from his grasp and sat back in the chair. "The Bible says a couple should not be unequally yoked, and we certainly would be."

"Unequally yoked? What kind of religious mumbo jumbo is that?" His ire seemed to be on the rise.

"It simply means that a believer should never pair off with an unbeliever."

"That is totally ridiculous! Believer, unbeliever. What difference does it make?" He turned his chair away from her and wheeled around to the opposite side of the room.

"It makes a world of difference to *me*!" She leapt out of the chair and stomped over to stand directly in front of him, hands on hips. "And what are you getting so angry about? You said yourself that you weren't ready for a relationship. Why should you care what *my* reasons are?"

"I'll show you why I should care," he growled, and before she realized what he was going to do, his hand shot up and caught her wrist. Jerking her onto his lap, he grasped her in his strong embrace and ferociously devoured her lips. Stasi squirmed and pushed against his shoulders, but he held fast. In a moment, his wrath seemed to dissipate as he softened the kiss. In spite of herself, Stasi couldn't resist the urge to coil her arms around his neck.

She suddenly came to her senses and pulled away. "Slade, stop," she said softly. "Don't make this any harder than it already is. For either of us."

He let out a frustrated sigh. "You're right. This is the second time I've had to apologize for kissing you, but I *am* sorry. It's just that . . . standing there with lightning flashing in those beautiful eyes . . ."

Still in his lap and his arms and feeling ridiculous, she pulled herself up into a straighter sitting position. "Why don't we just agree to remain very close friends for the time being? There's no rush. We have all the time in the world. If things should change in the future, we'll have another talk." Pushing herself from his lap, she said, "I think it's time for me to go." Then she headed for the door.

"Stasi, wait."

Stopping and turning, she moved toward him a few steps. "Yes?"

"I wasn't really angry with you. I'm angry at my situation and at myself. For things not being like they used to be and for not being able to be the kind of man you're looking for."

Remaining where she was, she replied, "It's not that you're not *able*, Slade. It's just the choice you made."

With that she swept out of his apartment, deciding what she was going to be fervently praying for. For however long it took.

CHAPTER THIRTY-ONE

SLADE HADN'T SEEN STASI FOR A FEW DAYS AFTER THAT NIGHT AT his apartment. She had made no effort to call or come over. But then, neither had he. No need to prolong the agony, he reasoned.

To keep Stasi off his mind, Slade began thinking about what he should do with the rest of his life. Would he be able to return to Conrad, Mitchell? Should he try working out of his apartment so that he wouldn't have to travel around with his wheelchair?

As these thoughts skipped around in his mind early one morning, he was jarred to reality by the phone ringing. Hoping it was Stasi, he wheeled across the living room at full speed.

"Hello?"

"Hello, Slade?"

He heard a slightly familiar male voice that he hadn't heard in a long time. Disappointed that it wasn't the voice he'd hoped to hear, he answered, "Yes? Who is this?"

"It's Darrell. Darrell Boyd."

"Darrell? Oh, yes. How are you?"

"I'm fine, but the question is, how are you?" He went on before Slade had a chance to answer. "I heard what happened with Troy, and all . . . Well, I just wanted to say I'm sorry about everything that's happened to you."

"Thanks. How are things going at the office?" He couldn't resist the urge to ask.

"Pretty well. I'm taking care of most of your clients now. Some have asked about you."

"That's good. About your taking care of my clients, I mean. I'm sure you're doing a fine job."

There was a short silence on the other end of the line, then Darrell asked, "You mean that, Slade?"

Slade shifted in the wheelchair. "Of course I mean it. Why wouldn't I?"

"I got the impression you thought my work was inferior to yours and the rest of the partners. I mean, after you voted me down for a partnership, I thought you didn't like me much, or that you were prejudiced against my race. That's why I never visited you in the hospital."

Slade expelled a heavy sigh into the phone. "Darrell, let me assure you. My decision to vote against you as a partner had nothing to do with your work, or the fact that you're black."

"It didn't?"

"No, it didn't. As a matter of fact, if either of those things had had any influence on me, you would never have been taken into the firm in the first place."

"I see what you mean, but what was the reason then?"

"I think your work is superb. I just felt that you weren't ready at that point in time. You were still a little green, and I thought you should have more experience before you were made partner. That's all there was to it. It didn't mean that I would never vote you in."

"Wow. I feel really stupid. All the resentment I harbored. . ."

"Don't worry about it, Darrell. It's forgotten. Let's just go on from here. Anyway, if I were there now, I would certainly recommend you for partner."

"Thanks, Slade. That means a lot to me."

"Listen, Darrell, why don't we get together for lunch one day soon?"

"Sure, that'd be great!"

"Would you mind picking me up at home? It seems I can't just hop in the old Jag and zoom off like I used to." He gave a weak laugh.

"No problem, buddy."

"Great. Since my schedule is pretty much clear all the time, you can give me a call when you feel it can be worked into yours."

"I'll do that. And soon."

Replacing the cordless phone in the base, Slade felt relief wash over him that the wall that loomed between the two men had been broken down. He had always been uncomfortable in the knowledge that Darrell resented him, but for the sake of the business, high standards came first.

The phone rang again, and Slade was afraid to even hope that it might be Stasi this time. But he did anyway.

Once again, his hopes were dashed when he was greeted by the voice of John Conrad.

"Slade. How are you, old buddy?"

"Just peachy, John," he replied dryly.

"Sorry, Slade. I didn't mean to sound so glib. Really, though, how are you?"

"All things considered, I could be a lot worse."

"You got that right."

Slade was getting fidgety. "Hold on, John. I have to get out of this wheelchair for a little while." He lifted himself out of the wheelchair and onto the couch. "Okay, that's better. So, where've you been?"

"Oh, uh, I've been busy going here and there, doing this and that." John's voice took on a defensive note, as if Slade were accusing him of something.

"Wow," Slade said, laughing. "Sounds interesting and fun."

"Right. Uh, Slade, before the accident you told me about a copy of a database file you made and took home. Do you remember at all?"

Slade briefly searched his memory. "Sorry, John. I don't remember."

"Could you have a look around your apartment when you have a few spare minutes? Maybe you labeled it."

"Sure, John, I'll look. What do you want it for?"

"I'd like to have a look at it. It seems the original file in the database was deleted, and the firm has to reimburse all those poor people who were taken in by Troy, you know."

"Oh, that's right. Well, as I said, I'll have a look around."

"Great. Oh, and Slade, let's do lunch sometime soon," he added noncommittally.

"Sure, John."

Well, that was certainly an odd conversation. You might think John called only to ask about that disk. In an instant, Slade was back in the chair and rolling toward his office. He rummaged through the drawers in his desk, but there was no disk just lying inside one of them. Then, realizing he should have gone to the obvious place, he reached for the disk file sitting on top of the desk and pulled it toward him.

In a scene that seemed oddly like deja vu, he found mostly gray disks, but one bright yellow one stood out. Fishing it out of the holder, he removed it from the sleeve and popped it into his computer drive. When he accessed the disk directory, he chose a document and pulled it up on the screen. It was a statement form for RDT Communications, a company he'd never heard of. Closing that document, he went back into the directory and chose another. This time a list appeared on the screen. Names, dates, and huge amounts of money. From somewhere deep in the recesses of his consciousness, he vaguely recalled seeing this list before. Also familiar was the growing apprehension welling up inside him from the pit of his stomach.

This was the disk that John had asked him to find. Without knowing why, he felt uncomfortable with the thought of just handing it over. What should he do? Should he give it to John and forget about it? Or should he keep it awhile longer until he knew more?

He needed to talk to someone, needed advice on how best to proceed. And he knew exactly where to go.

A minute later, he was across the hall, ringing Stasi's doorbell. The door opened, and there she stood: pale, drowsy-eyed, tousled hair, wearing baggy sweats. She held a crumpled tissue to her runny nose. Her eyes reflected a brief hint of shock at seeing him there that quickly faded.

"What happened to *you*?" he asked

"I cawd a code." Leaving the door open, she scuffed her way over to the couch and dropped herself into a horizontal position.

Slade rolled through the door, closed it, then proceeded over to the couch and touched his palm to her forehead. "You have a fever, too."

"I doe."

"Have you taken anything?"

"Dot yet. Just god up."

"I'm sorry, did I wake you?"

"Doe."

"Do you have aspirin in your medicine cabinet?"

"Yeah."

"Hold on." Slade went into the bathroom and rummaged through her medicine cabinet, trying to ignore all the feminine toiletries placed strategically around the room. This was something he would have normally liked to explore further, recalling the old saying that implies going through a person's medicine cabinet tells a lot about the person. He suddenly had an inexplicable longing to know Stasi more intimately. Not just knowing things like what kind of cologne she wore or what color lipstick she preferred, but he wanted tangibles. He wanted to take that bottle of fragrance she spritzed on every day and spray it into the air, sniffing its contents—to take that hairbrush and run it through her long, silky locks.

He should stop this. Stasi would most likely be offended if she knew he was having these thoughts about her, though he wasn't applying them to Stasi in the same regard that he used to for other women. It was more out of affection.

Oh, he didn't know what it was. He only knew it wasn't the same thing.

Locating the aspirin and a bottle of cold medicine, he pulled in a deep breath. His nostrils were immediately filled with the scent of a blend of vanilla, lemons, and wildflowers.

He needed to get out of here before he lost his mind. Back in the living room, Slade asked Stasi if she had orange juice, which she did. He poured her a glass and handed it to her with a capful of cold medicine and two aspirin. "Drink the orange juice down, Stasi," he ordered in his best doctor's voice. "The vitamin C will do you good."

"Thang you," she mumbled, handing him the empty glass. Then she twisted into a fetal position and closed her eyes.

Slade stared resignedly at her unmoving form. He knew she wasn't up to talking now. After placing the empty juice glass on the end table by the couch, he wheeled to her bedroom. It seemed to him a totally feminine sanctuary. The colors were a perfect blend of dusty rose and white, with splashes of gray here and there. The room was adorned with lacy curtains and a ruffled bedspread with a heap of frilly pillows piled on top of the bed. The bureau and night tables were accented with lace doilies and fancy curios.

Spotting a folded blanket on a white wicker chair in the corner, he lifted it off. The same vanilla fragrance wafted to his nostrils as it had in the bathroom. Going over to the bed, he dug under the pile for a bed pillow. She wouldn't want to use one of the fancy ones, he felt sure. Stacking these things on his lap, he headed back to the living room.

Stasi appeared to be sleeping soundly. He gently lifted her head, placing the pillow underneath, then lightly covered her with the blanket. She snuggled into the comfort, a satisfied smile adorning her features.

Just as Slade was about to turn the wheelchair and leave, he heard her mumble something. "I thought you were asleep," he said.

"Barely."

"What did you say before?"

"Could you pud da glass in da kidgen singk? Don'd wand rings on by table."

He couldn't repress a smile. Even in sickness, she had to have everything perfect. "Sure, no problem." After doing so, he moved toward the door and said, "I'll see you later, Stasi."

"Could use sub cobady," she mumbled, barcly audible and with her eyes still closed.

"You want me to stay while you sleep?"

"Mmm-hmm."

"I'd be glad to," he replied, wheeling over to the couch. "Now you get some rest," he told her, smoothing her hair back from her face. "I'll be right here."

Three hours later, Stasi woke refreshed and feeling somewhat better, though her sinuses were still a little stuffy. She peered over the blanket and caught a glimpse of Slade sitting in his wheelchair a few feet away, reading a book. Staring hard, her vision focused after a moment, and she was amazed to see that the book was her Bible. She recalled leaving it on the end table the previous night.

"You're reading my Bible." This was said more to convince herself than for any other purpose.

Her clear voice cutting through the silence must have startled him, because his head snapped up as he clapped the Good Book closed. "Yes, for want of something better to do." He placed the Bible on a nearby table. "Feeling better?"

She stretched lazily. "Yes, much. I'm sorry you were so bored, but thanks for staying."

"It's the least I could do. I heated up a can of chicken noodle soup a little while ago. It's still warm. Would you like some?"

"Sure, that'd be great."

She started to push the blanket aside, as if to get up, but Slade stopped her. "Where do you think you're going?"

Puzzled, she looked up at him. "To get my soup. Where do you think?"

"You stay right there. I'll get it." He rolled into the kitchen.

Stasi listened to the clink of dishes and utensils, a drawer opening and closing, metal scraping against metal as he emptied the soup from the pan into a bowl with a spoon.

Hoisting herself into a sitting position, she looked up to view the one thing about Slade's condition that always punctured her heart with torment. He came toward her, bearing the bowl of soup in his hands like a prize. Holding her breath and suppressing the tremendous urge to spring to his assistance, she forced herself to wait patiently while his every precise, drawn-out step became an eternity before he and his wheelchair were finally before her. Slowly releasing her pent-up breath, she reached for the bowl.

"Ah-ah-ah," he admonished, sweeping it gently out of her range. Taking up the spoon, he scooped up the soup and held it and the bowl under her chin. "Open wide."

"Slade, you're crazy! I can feed myself."

"I know it, but just humor me. Act as if *you* need *me* for a change."

She winced and turned her face aside.

"C'mon, Stasi, the soup's getting cold. Just allow me this one simple pleasure."

"I feel like a child," she said, but obliged by opening her mouth.

"I know the feeling," he said, his tone flat.

Would she never learn to be careful what she said to him? "I'm sorry. I didn't think."

"Forget it. You can't walk on eggshells all the time, but if some things remind me about my situation, I might just say the first thing that comes to mind." He picked up a napkin from his lap and dabbed at a dribble of broth on her chin. "Let's not worry about what we say. We each know the other well enough to understand our intentions, so let's just speak off the tops of our heads, as we always did."

She studied his face. It was relaxed, resigned. "Okay, Slade." She took the bowl from him. "I appreciate your being here. Thanks."

"Don't mention it."

After slurping down a few spoonfuls, she looked up at him expectantly. "I'm sure you had a reason for coming over."

"Uh, yeah, I did." He shoved his hair back off his forehead, then explained the call from John, finding the disk, and the information he had found on it. "I was hoping you could help me figure out what to do next," he said after finishing the story.

Reaching back, she placed the empty soup bowl on the end table, careful to make sure her napkin was underneath. "Aren't you going to give the disk to John?"

"I don't know if I should."

"Why not? He's like a father to you, isn't he? Your mentor?"

He shifted in the chair and placed his elbows on the armrests. "Yes, but I just have this gut feeling. I don't know what it is, but since the incident with Troy, I just don't know who I can trust anymore."

Stasi focused on the lamp across the room and thought for a moment. "This is what we'll do: keep the disk for a while. John doesn't have to know you found it. Then we'll see if we can come up with some other information before deciding whether to hand it over."

Slade nodded. "Sounds like a plan. But how do we get this 'other' information?"

Crossing her arms, she pinned him with a knowing gaze. "Slade, you forget that you are talking to the 'Queen of Information.'"

Slade's eyes sparkled with humor as he doubled over in his chair, executing a near-perfect salaam. "My humble apologies, Your Majesty."

Stasi giggled. "Okay, seriously. Get me all the personal information you can, not only on John but also on any other partners. Then. . ."

"Hold it!" He held his hand up in a halting gesture. "I thought *you* were supposed to come up with the information."

She rolled her eyes. "No, silly. I need *personal* information to gain access to *background* information. If anyone has any secrets, *that's* where it's usually hidden."

He nodded. "I see. But what kind of personal info are you talking about?"

"Easy stuff. Birthdates, Social Security numbers, bank account numbers, if you're privy to them."

"Okay, I'll do my best to get it all together for you." Remaining where he was, he stared at her, his gaze penetrating. She detected something there that she couldn't pinpoint. Was it admiration? Affection? *Love*?

"What?" she asked at his continued staring.

He seemed to snap out of whatever trance he was in. "Oh! Uh, it's just that . . . I knew I could count on you." Drawing nearer, he kissed her forehead. "Thanks." Then he wheeled toward the door.

"Where are you going?"

"To get started. I'll have to enlist Arlene's help."

"Oh," she said to the closing door.

CHAPTER THIRTY-TWO

WEDNESDAY AFTERNOON BEFORE THANKSGIVING, SLADE'S mother was due to arrive from Florida for the holidays, and Stasi offered to take Slade and pick her up at the airport in Philadelphia. They watched the passengers stream out of the terminal, when Slade finally said, "There she is." He pointed to a slight, short brunette, tan and well-dressed. Her hair was neatly clipped in short layers, accentuating the same classic features Stasi saw in Slade's face. Stasi didn't know about Slade's father, but she could easily see that his mother contributed a great part to his good looks.

"Over here, Mom!" he called.

"Son! Oh, Slade!" Lois Mitchell ran to her son, bending over to wrap her arms around his neck. Tears were streaming down her well made-up cheeks when she pulled away from him. "Look at you!" she moaned, moving her dark eyes over him. "Oh, Slade!" she said again and clutched him to her tightly.

"Mom, Mom, whoa!" he said, pulling her arms from around his neck. "It's okay. I'm okay." He cleared his throat and motioned toward Stasi. "Mom, this is Stasi. You remember, you spoke with her on the phone."

"Oh, yes," Lois said, clasping the hand Stasi offered. "I'm glad to finally meet you."

On closer inspection, Stasi could see a light sprinkling of gray throughout the older woman's dark hair and crow's-feet at the outer corners of her eyes. "I'm pleased to meet you too, Ms. Mitchell."

"Oh, please, let's dispense with the formalities. Call me Lois."

"Okay, Lois."

"Stasi, we'd better get Mom's luggage and get out of here."

They collected the two small suitcases Lois had brought and were soon on their way over the bridge, and back into New Jersey.

In the car, Lois sat in the back seat weeping softly.

"Mom, what's the matter? Why are you crying?"

"Oh, Slade, I just can't get used to seeing you this way. You always seemed so . . .," she searched for the right words, "larger than life. So virile."

"Mom, please. Don't do this. Don't cry anymore. I'm still me."

"Okay, son. I'll try," she said, still sniffing.

"It's a good thing I *didn't* let you see me after the accident. You'd have fallen apart."

This set off a whole new torrent of tears and wails from Lois.

"Mom!" he pleaded, drawing the word out.

"Sorry, Slade."

Back at the apartment building, Lois insisted on helping Slade out of the car and into his wheelchair.

"Mom, please, I'm used to doing it myself."

"I'm sorry, Slade. I don't mean to be this way. I know how independent you are. I promise to try to restrain myself from now on."

Once inside Slade's apartment, Stasi addressed Lois. "I had an idea that Slade agrees with."

"Yes?"

"Since Slade uses his extra room as an office, you can stay at my apartment. I have a guest room all set up."

"Oh, honey, I don't want to impose. I can sleep here on the sofa." She walked over and tentatively perched on the edge of the cold leather furniture.

"No, really, no imposition. We had it all planned. I'd love to have you. And you'll be just across the hall from Slade. You can come and go as you please."

Lois got up from the couch. "Well, if you're sure," she said, looking down at the sofa in distaste.

"Positive. Come on, I'll show you your room."

The two women left Slade's apartment chattering and laughing like two teenage schoolgirls.

After Stasi and his mother left his apartment, Slade marveled at the kindness of this woman, who never ceased to amaze him. She gave of herself without reserve. No gimmicks, no ulterior motives. All heart. She was there for him at every turn, even taking his mother in at the expense of her own convenience and privacy.

Was this what it meant to be a Christian? Never to think of oneself but always to think of others?

Man, he wished he could reach that level of selflessness.

And he wished he could be the kind of man Stasi deserved in every way. Physically, emotionally, and spiritually.

Stasi prepared a light supper of vegetable soup and grilled cheese sandwiches at her apartment for Slade and Lois. Afterward, the three lingered around the table over coffee and cookies while Lois entertained Stasi with stories of Slade's childhood financial endeavors.

"Even at the tender age of nine, Slade was somewhat of a financial wizard. He saw opportunity in everything."

Slade rolled his eyes, apparently embarrassed. "Mom, please."

"I'm sorry, son, but I must give credit where it is due," she told him with mock indignance. "Now, where was I?" Her eyes shifted upward as she thought. "Oh, yes. Well, as I said, he saw opportunity in everything. One day, he and I were shopping on Broadway in Camden when he spotted a dollar bill lying on the pavement." Lois smiled proudly, lost in the long-ago memory. "He was so excited because he had found a whole dollar. But after a few minutes, he began to wonder how he could turn that dollar into more. Well, soon we turned onto Federal Street, stopping to look into the window of Woolworth's. That's when he saw the shoeshine kit. The price was seven-fifty. He looked down at the dollar bill, then back at the shoeshine kit, then smiled and tugged me into the store. I asked him how he was going to buy that with only one dollar, since I didn't have the money to lend him the rest. All he said was, 'You'll see.'

"Instead of heading for the kit, he went to the craft department and picked up two packages of felt lettering that were on sale for fifty cents each. I did give him the extra few cents for tax.

"He took those letters and went to the neighborhood kids, offering to put their gang name on the backs of their jackets for a dollar each." Here she paused and, shooting Stasi a meaningful glance, waved her hand, saying, "All the kids in Camden City back then belonged to gangs. Even the young ones."

"They still do," Slade contributed.

"Anyway, getting back to the story, Slade made eleven dollars. More than enough to buy that shoeshine kit! And when he did, he went over to City Hall every day with it, which was an excellent place for business, what with all those lawyers and government workers."

Stasi looked at Slade. "I'm impressed! No wonder you're so successful today."

Slade shrugged, having the grace to look humble.

"But the best part was," Lois continued, pushing her coffee cup aside, "that he started a bank account and saved every penny he made shining shoes. That was the start of his saving for college. After saving everything he made from every little job he had, he had a nice bundle stored up by the time he was old enough, I can tell you," she finished, a typically proud mother.

"That's a wonderful story!" Stasi said, clasping her hands to her chest. "Slade, I had no idea you were so resourceful."

"Stick around," he said with a wink.

It was getting late, and they all had to get up early in the morning. Lois cleared the table while Stasi loaded the dishwasher. Slade decided it was time he went back to his own apartment, though he was hesitant to leave the enveloping warmth that had developed. Here was his mother, whom he loved immensely, getting along with his good friend as if she were a part of the family. Stasi, on the other hand, took his mother into her own home as if she'd known her for years.

They were the two most important women in his life.

He said good night and wheeled across to his own empty apartment. As soon as he passed through the door, he felt as though he had left behind a very integral part of himself.

After changing into their nightclothes, Stasi and Lois spent a few quiet moments before going to bed. Lounging on the sofa, they engaged in some typical girl talk. But then Lois steered the conversation toward Slade, bringing up the very subject that Stasi considered tabu at this point in time.

"Stasi, honey, I can see by the way that you and Slade look at each other that there's something between you. Yet the two of you are determined to act as if you are only good friends. I hope you don't mind my asking, but what's keeping the two of you apart?"

"I . . . uh . . . well . . ."

"I know," Lois cut in. "It's really none of my business, but Slade's my son, and I only want to see him happy." She studied Stasi's face curiously. "Right now, you seem to be the very thing that would make him happy."

Stasi sighed, relenting. "Okay, Lois, I'll be honest with you, though I'm not sure how Slade would feel about my confiding in you about it."

Lois placed her hand on Stasi's arm, an understanding gesture. "I won't tell if you won't. And what he doesn't know won't hurt him."

A shy smile spread across Stasi's lips. "The truth is, Slade and I do care for each other, but it's just impossible for us to be anything more than just friends. At least, for the moment."

"But why?"

"Well, you see, I'm a born-again Christian, and. . ."

"No!"

She was taken aback at Lois's sudden outburst. "Well, yes," she said a little shakily. "And . . ."

"Oh, Stasi, this is wonderful!"

"It is?" she asked, incredulous.

Lois was laughing and practically bouncing up and down with excitement. "Of course! You see, I'm a Christian, too."

Now it was Stasi's turn. "No!"

"Yes, isn't this terrific?"

"Well, yes, but it doesn't change the fact that Slade is still an unbeliever." She became sorrowful at the thought. "You must know we couldn't let things go any further."

"Don't worry about Slade. I have complete faith that the Holy Spirit will do a work in him soon."

Stasi smiled. "I hope you're right." Then something dawned on her. "Slade doesn't know, does he?"

Lois drew in a long, slow breath before answering. "No, I haven't had a chance to tell him. It happened several months ago, and as you know, I couldn't get through to him."

Stasi nodded in acknowledgment.

"We'll tell him tomorrow," Lois said with what seemed like false confidence. "But right now, I think we'd better hit the sack. We have a long day tomorrow."

"Right. Good night, Lois," Stasi said as they both stood up.

The two women hugged before entering their separate rooms.

On Thanksgiving morning, everyone was up and bustling by seven. Stasi already had the turkey stuffed and in the oven, and Lois had a spice cake baking over at Slade's. The three of them happily flitted from one apartment to the other as the holiday preparations got under way with the precision of a Swiss clock.

By three in the afternoon, Stasi's dining table was set with her own fine china that Slade secretly believed rivaled his own set on which he had served her dinner a few weeks ago. He had been in charge of the salad and mixed vegetables and was just placing them on the table when Lois added a plate of cranberry sauce along with a large bowl containing a curious-looking orange concoction.

"What's that, Mom?"

"Whipped sweet potatoes. Wait'll you try them. They'll knock your socks off! I got the recipe from a friend of mine down in Florida. You know, the food is just delicious down there."

"Looks good." Slade leaned in and sniffed. "Smells good, too."

Stasi went to the kitchen, returned balancing the steaming, plump turkey on a serving platter that seemed wider than her waistline, and carefully lowered it to the table.

"Why don't we pray first, and then Slade can carve the turkey?" Lois suggested.

Slade threw his mother a curious glance.

"Would you do the honors, Lois?" Stasi asked.

They sat at the table and bowed their heads while Lois concocted an elaborate prayer as if it were old hat. After they had all said amen, Slade stared at his mother, incredulous. "Mom?"

The two women exchanged knowing glances before Lois answered. "Yes, son?"

"You did that like an old pro." He drew the words out, unsure of what to expect in response.

Lois was sitting to the left of Slade, and Stasi to his right, forming a half-circle. Lois reached over and took his hand in both of hers. "I haven't had a chance to tell you before," she began softly, "but I've become a born-again Christian."

Sighing heavily, Slade bowed his head and covered his eyes with his free hand. In the next instant, his whole body was shaking.

"Slade, what's wrong?" Lois sounded frightened.

"Slade?" Stasi stammered.

He slowly raised his head, revealing the wetness around his eyes. He guessed they couldn't tell he'd been laughing.

"Slade, what's going on?" Lois's voice had a tinge of anger to it.

He moved his head back and forth. "Mom, it's just so ironic. First, it was just Stasi, but now . . . well, it looks as though I'm outnumbered!"

Lois's mouth gave way to a slow, apprehensive smile. "You're not upset?"

He leaned over and kissed her cheek. "Of course not. I've been living in close proximity to a Christian all this time who just happens to be a wonderful woman." He glanced at Stasi admiringly, then turned back to his mother and continued. "I'm used to it. But now, the two most important women in my life have something in common, and I think it's great."

"Oh, Slade," was all she could say.

Stasi smiled.

"Now, let's eat. I'm starved!" he said, reaching for the carving knife.

Later, after the dinner dishes had been washed and put away, Stasi, Slade, and Lois relaxed in the living room.

"So tell me, Mom. How did this conversion of yours come about?"

Lois removed her shoes and curled her feet under her on the couch. "It was during the time when you had your accident and I couldn't get through to you. After a while, I was not only worried but also extremely anxious. Then a neighbor of mine, Millie, who is a Christian, suggested it might help if I turned to God."

"Sounds familiar," Slade mumbled, throwing Stasi a cursory glance.

Stasi shot back a wide-eyed, "so what?" look.

"I scoffed at first," Lois continued. "I didn't believe that God would be concerned with my little problem with all of the more important issues in the world that needed tending to. But then Millie offered to sit down with me to explain God's plan of salvation and show me where in the Bible it is stated in Jesus' own words. After that, I felt in my heart that I really needed to accept God's grace through His Son, Jesus Christ."

"That simple, huh?

"That simple," Lois reiterated. "If it weren't for my faith, I don't know how I would have gotten through all those months when I hadn't heard a word from you."

"Sorry for that, Mom," was all he could say. But what he was thinking was that if his mother believed, it might be something worth looking into.

Midmorning on Friday, Slade was just about to join Stasi and his mother at Stasi's apartment when his doorbell rang. Wondering why either of the women would ring the bell, he was surprised to find John Conrad standing there when he opened the door. "John! How are you?"

"Great, Slade. How are things with you?"

"Not so bad," he answered, waving John in, then turning and wheeling into the living room.

"You look terrific!"

John said this with such an inflection that Slade got the impression that John was not only surprised to find him in such good shape but also a little disappointed. "Thanks. I feel terrific. Now what can I do for you?"

"*Do* for me?" He frowned as if Slade should know better. "Don't you think I can visit my young protégé without some ulterior motive? Come on, Slade, you've been like a son to me all these years."

That was laying it on a little thick. "I guess so," Slade answered, thinking of all the time he spent in the hospital without seeing John more than once or twice.

"But now that you mention it," John began wryly, "I was wondering if you'd ever come across that missing disk."

He hated lying to John, but he didn't feel comfortable handing that disk over to him just yet. Besides, he was waiting for that report. "No, I haven't." He also knew he needed time to figure out this instinctive, unsettling sentiment gnawing at his insides.

"I see."

"I was just about to join my mother who is staying at a friend's across the hall. Would you care to join us for some coffee?"

"Of course. For a little while."

When Slade and John entered the apartment, the two women were in the kitchen chatting. Stasi was preparing the coffee, and Lois sat at the table.

"Stasi, Mom, this is John Conrad, my friend and one of my business partners."

John took the hand that Stasi offered. "Glad to meet you. I've heard how you've been there for Slade, and I think it's wonderful."

"Thank you, Mr. Conrad."

"John. Please." He turned to Lois, and his eyes took on a glint of absorbed interest. "Lois." He took her hand and raised her out of the chair. "*May* I call you Lois?" He went on when she nodded. "I'm so glad to meet you. Why has Slade kept such an attractive lady hidden all these years?"

Lois blushed girlishly, practically swooning.

Slade wanted to puke. He'd seen John pour on the sweetness for clients, but . . . his mother?

It turned out that John spent more than "a little while" with them, and he ended up having lunch there, too. He listened with rapt attention whenever Lois spoke, as if no one else were in the room.

John finally decided to leave at about two-thirty. On his way to the door, he stopped and turned to Lois. "Would you like to have dinner and take in a movie with me tomorrow night?"

"Oh, I . . . I'm in town to visit with Slade for the holidays," she stammered, then glanced at Slade with a question in her eyes.

Slade reluctantly let her off the hook. "That's okay, Mom. There's no reason for you to be here every minute. Go out and have a good time."

She turned back to John, eagerness lacing her response. "In that case, I'd love to, John."

He smiled engagingly. "Good. I'll pick you up at six."

Lois walked John to the door and, after closing it behind him, turned to Slade with a dreamy look. "You didn't tell me your partner was so handsome!"

"Well, gee, Mom," he shot back with a sardonic frown, "I hadn't really noticed."

"Now, now, be nice, Slade," she said. "You're sure you don't mind my going out with him?"

After seeing the predatory gleam in John's eyes, he really did mind, but he wanted her focused on herself for a change. "Mom, you'll be here for a month. There will be plenty of time for us to be together. I want you to enjoy yourself."

She walked over and placed a quick kiss on his cheek. "Thanks, son."

Lois retired to her room early that night while Slade and Stasi lingered on the living room sofa. Slade had seemed a little pre-occupied since John left, and Stasi asked him about it.

"Slade, what's wrong? You haven't seemed yourself since John was here."

He heaved a deep sigh and shook his head. "I don't know, Stasi. I just don't feel comfortable around John anymore. And I'm not at all sure I like the idea of my mother going out with him."

"But this is the man who taught you everything you know. A man who was like a father to you. I thought the two of you were close."

"I know, it seems crazy, but ever since the accident, and especially finding out about Troy . . ." He shrugged. "I guess I'm just afraid to trust anyone after everything that's happened."

"Who can blame you? Two attempts have been made on your life, and a trusted friend and business partner turned out to be *un*trustworthy."

He smiled and reached for her hand. "At least there's one person I know I can always trust. Thanks, Stasi. For everything. I don't know how I'll ever make it up to you."

"There's nothing to make up for. I wanted to do it." She paused for a moment. "Don't be too hasty in your distrust of John. After all, you've known him for years, and I'd hate to see your relationship with him ruined because of what Troy did to you."

"You're right," he concurred, kissing the hand he still held. "I guess I'm being super paranoid. I'll try not to jump to conclusions about him without any hard evidence."

And Stasi would try not to jump to conclusions about the tingling sensation Slade's kiss left on her hand.

CHAPTER THIRTY-THREE

JUST BEFORE SIX O'CLOCK ON SATURDAY, LOIS EMERGED from Stasi's guest room. Slade had never seen his mother looking more beautiful. This worried him, but he wasn't about to analyze it after his talk with Stasi the night before.

Stasi got up from the couch and walked over to Lois. "Lois, you look stunning." She turned to Slade. "Doesn't she, Slade?"

He had to agree. She could pass for a woman ten years younger than fifty-one. Tonight, she wore a salmon silk skirt suit with a frothy white hand-crocheted top. Her short, dark hair was done up into a fullness he'd never seen before. Her face glowed with the anticipation of a young girl about to go on her first date.

And he felt like that girl's father. He was worried about John's intentions and didn't want to see his mother hurt. The intensity with which John had gazed at Lois yesterday had disturbed him.

The sound of the doorbell yanked him into the present. He was sitting in his wheelchair next to the sofa and remained where he was when Stasi let John in.

John nodded in his direction. "Slade."

"John." Apparently, Lois had gone back into the guest room, as she was nowhere to be seen.

"I hope you don't mind my taking your mother out for an evening," John said to him.

Slade immediately felt guilty. Obviously, no matter how hard he tried to hide his sentiments, they still came through. "Of course not, John. It will be good for her to get out."

"Great, because I thought I detected some apprehension on your part."

"I guess I'm just being a little overprotective of my mom. You know how it is."

John nodded just as Lois made her second entrance that evening. He immediately walked over to her, took both her hands in his. "Lois, you're beautiful."

Lois's reply was lost to Slade, who was too busy noticing that same glint in John's eye that he had seen yesterday when he first introduced them.

Lois came over and gave Slade a brief peck on the forehead. "I'll see you kids later. Don't wait up."

Slade jerked his head up to look at her. "How late are you going to be?"

She shot John a conspiratorial glance. "I don't know. It depends on how much fun we're having," she answered with a giggle.

His throat went dry.

His resolution not to be distrusting went right out the window.

Since Lois was out with John for the evening, Slade and Stasi decided to order a pizza and watch a video at her apartment. She helped him onto the couch, removed his shoes, and arranged his stockinged feet on the coffee table. After setting up the VCR, Stasi settled next to Slade and handed him a slice of pizza on a paper plate.

They ate and watched in silence for a short while until Slade asked her to hand him a napkin. As he drew the napkin across his mouth, Stasi noticed that he had left a spot of pizza sauce on his chin. On impulse, she took another napkin from the coffee table. As she leaned over to wipe the spot away, his intense gaze locked with hers, causing a quickening deep in the pit of her stomach. Taking her delicate hand in his large, warm one, he squeezed it, crushing the napkin inside.

"Stasi." His voice was deep and low, hinting at volumes of unspoken words.

She didn't respond, at least not outwardly. Instead, she pulled her hand free and turned away, flicking the crumpled napkin onto the table in front of her. Why did it keep coming to moments like this? But then, what did she expect? She wasn't sure she had the strength to maintain their friendship and keep it at that when every time she got near him all her defenses seemed to fall away. She didn't know whether she could go on like this indefinitely.

Finally realizing there was no denying it, she allowed herself to form the words in her mind: *I'm in love with him.*

That's it. There was no joy, no fanfare in her heart. It was a forbidden love, and she had allowed herself to give in to it.

Slade reached for her and turned her toward him again. Eyes brimming with unasked questions, he gently pulled her closer, surprising her with his strength. When he tenderly touched his lips to hers, she knew he was her weakness and that she'd be battling it for a long time to come.

The kiss ended, and she looked at him through a blur of unshed tears. "Slade, this is wrong. You know it, and I know it."

"I don't know any such thing. The only thing coming between us is your faith."

A brief thought flitted through her mind that more than that came between them.

She tried to pull out of his embrace, but he wouldn't let her. "Sweetheart, let's just enjoy the moment. No strings attached." He kissed her again.

No strings. That sounded like the old Slade. It didn't matter, though. She forced herself to relax and, hating herself, admitted she was right where she longed to be: in Slade's arms.

Yes, he was her weakness. This man, who didn't see himself as a whole man because of his physical challenges and tried to over-compensate in other areas.

This man. The only man besides Barry she'd ever love but could never have.

In the blanket of darkness, Stasi glanced at the illuminated red numbers on the clock radio. Three-fifteen. Lois had come home from her date with John over two hours ago, and Slade had left shortly after.

She twisted onto her side, clutching one of the pillows to her chest. This was killing her. What had she been thinking when she offered to help Slade after the accident? Kindness was uppermost in her mind at the time, but had she subconsciously harbored ulterior motives for her actions?

Despite knowing what kind of person he was, the kind of life he led, she had always liked him. Regardless of his morals—or lack of—she could never have turned away from him. Or anyone, for that matter. Yet for some reason she couldn't put her finger on, she had always been drawn to Slade. Of course, so were hundreds of other women. But for her, it went way beyond his charm and good looks. For all his roguish ways, she felt that Slade wore them as a protective covering, beneath was a more honorable and vulnerable man. And *that* was the man she had fallen in love with.

Realization smacked her hard in the face. She had been well on her way to falling for Slade long before the accident!

Squeezing her eyes shut tight, the tears seeped through. *Father, forgive me for my sin against You by allowing myself to become entangled in this relationship. I pray that You will guide my path as I leave it in Your hands.*

On Sunday, Stasi and Lois attended the late service, so Slade didn't see them until lunchtime. When they arrived home, he called them over to his apartment, where he had prepared the fixings for bacon, lettuce, and tomato sandwiches.

They made some small talk as they ate, but Slade finally got around to the subject he really wanted to discuss.

"It was too late to talk when you got home last night, but how did your date with John go, Mom?"

Lois laughed. "Oh Slade, really! It wasn't actually a date."

"What would you call it then?"

"Oh, well . . ." she groped for words. "It was just two people who enjoy each other's company going out together."

Slade took a bite of his sandwich. "Mm-hmm." He chewed, then swallowed. "But how did it go?"

Lois put her sandwich down on the plate none too gently. "Honestly, Slade! What do you want me to say? It was fine. We had a nice time."

"I'm sorry, Mom," he said, feeling stupid. "It's just that I'm a little worried about his intentions toward you."

"Perhaps he hasn't *any* intentions toward me except to enjoy my company while I'm in town." She frowned, studying him for a few seconds. "Why are you so worried about it? I thought he was a good friend."

Slade shrugged. "I don't know. I guess it's different when it's your own mother. Besides, he's been married and divorced three times. I don't want you becoming casualty number four."

Lois rolled her eyes. "Oh, really!"

Slade continued. "And aren't Christians supposed to stay away from romantic relationships with unbelievers?" He turned to Stasi now, who had been quietly observing the whole conversation. "You know, Stasi, that unequally yoked thing we discussed. Remind her, will you?"

"I, uh . . ." she stammered. "It's none of my business."

"Slade, look at me," Lois demanded. When he did, she went on. "First of all, I know all about being unequally yoked. Second, you're getting carried away with this whole thing. Who said anything about romance or marriage? I'm not going to be here long enough for any of that."

Well, she'd certainly told him. He felt like a schoolboy after such a set down.

"We're just two people who enjoy each other's company," Lois continued. "Besides, John could use a little companionship, since he's been alone for so long, and if I can provide him with some while I'm here, then so be it."

Slade sipped his soft drink. "I'm sorry, Mom." He raised his hands in surrender. "You're right. I am getting carried away. I'll try to contain myself from now on."

Lois got up from her chair and kissed her son's forehead, then rubbed it clear of her lipstick remnants. "Good, because John's picking me up in half an hour. We're going to the mall and then to dinner. I suggest that while I'm out, you work on getting your own love life in order." She swept away from the table, leaving Slade to gape at the bedroom door she'd just breezed through.

A moment later, Lois flitted back into the room, holding her hand to her chest, and headed towards the coffee table where she had left her purse. Rummaging through it, she pulled out a pill bottle, twisted off the cap, and shook a pill into her palm. Slade was flabbergasted. He hadn't known his mother had any medical problems.

"Mom? What's the matter? What is that medicine for?"

She looked at him, apparently flustered. "Oh, these?" she asked, holding up the vial, her voice shaky.

"Yes, those."

"It's nothing, really. They're nitroglycerin tablets."

He was scared. He'd never thought of what he'd do if anything ever happened to his mother. "Nitroglycerin? Isn't that used for heart problems?"

"Well, yes. I have a little angina, and . . ."

"Angina! Mom, why didn't you tell me?"

"Because I knew you'd react exactly the way you're reacting. Besides, you have your own problems. I didn't want to bother you with my ailments."

"Bother me? *Bother me?*" He felt his face heating up like a steam iron. "How could you think that way? You're my mother. I have a right to know."

Lois wasn't flustered anymore. She drew herself up self-righteously. "I understand exactly how you feel. I'm sorry."

Slade hung his head. She'd never let him forget how he'd kept her in the dark about his accident. "Sorry, Mom." He looked up. "I guess we're two of a kind."

"That we are, son," she said, placing the tablet under her tongue and heading back to the bedroom.

After Lois left with John, Slade parked his wheelchair beside the sofa.

"Would you like me to turn on the TV?" Stasi offered, standing next to him.

"No, I don't feel much like watching television."

"What would you like to do?" she asked as she stepped toward the sofa.

He caught her hand just before she sat down and pulled her onto his lap. It was the only way he could speak with her eye to eye. "I thought we'd take my mother's suggestion." He slowly moved his lips toward hers, but she stopped him with a firm hand on his chest.

"I don't think this is what she had in mind."

"C'mon, Stasi, what happened to living for the moment? What harm could a few kisses do?"

She reached out and smoothed his hair off his forehead. "Plenty. And as for 'living for the moment,' I'm sorely tempted to just throw caution to the wind. But I can't, and what would be the point?"

"Pleasure. I like kissing you, and I *think*, you like kissing me."

Her full lips spread into a wistful smile. "I do. I like it very much. Too much." She moved off his lap and onto the sofa. "But where is it leading?"

"It doesn't have to lead anywhere. No strings, right?"

Rubbing her hands together hard, she clasped them, then looked at him with round, soulful eyes. "I'm sorry, but that doesn't work for me. You see, I *want* strings. If I'm with someone, it has to be because there's hope for a future together. I want to have the freedom to express what's in my heart, not suppress it because I'm afraid it will create strings."

Slade turned and wheeled to the other side of the room, leaving his back to her. "Stasi, as much as I'd like to, I can't give you that. Not like . . . this," he finished, gesturing to his own body. "You deserve better. Someone who's a man in every way. I could never be that for you."

Suddenly she was beside his wheelchair, on her knees and looking up at him. "Why can't you believe me when I tell you that physical abilities don't matter? Inside, you're very much a man."

He stared down at her. Could she be right? Likely she was the only woman to feel that way. But could he just act as though he had no infirmities and free himself to live life to the fullest? She was honest to a fault, so he knew she meant every word. With her, he *could* forget he was a cripple. She made him forget, made him feel he was every ounce the man he was before this happened to him.

But there was still the other thing between them.

"Okay, Stasi, say I act like there was nothing physically wrong with me. I pursue all my desires, you being one of them. What about *your* reason for holding back? Are you willing to forget I'm an unbeliever?"

Standing up, she walked to the other side of the room. "I couldn't do that."

Anger building, he swung the wheelchair around and rolled toward her. "Why not? Do you mean to tell me that you could deal with all the baggage attached to my situation, but because I don't share your religious beliefs you're willing to throw it all away?"

Unshed tears pooled in her eyes, giving them more sparkle. "Slade, please understand. I can't compromise my faith. God is the most important thing in my life. I won't disobey His commands."

Heart beating fast and getting desperate, he thought for a moment. Within the past few seconds, he had come to realize that he loved Stasi and was willing to do anything to have her. "What if I went to church with you, prayed with you, read the Bible? Would that be enough?"

Brimming tears finally spilled over like a cascading waterfall. "It would be a start, but . . ." Covering her wet face with her hands, she sunk onto the sofa.

Wheeling closer, he gently took her hands from her face and wiped the tears away with the edge of his shirtsleeve. "Wouldn't that be enough?" he asked again softly.

The pain in her eyes tore at his heart. "Slade, I won't lie, so, no, it's not enough. You should seek God only because it's *your* desire, not mine. He knows your heart, and if it isn't true, then you're not really saved."

The anger returned, mixed with hurt, and he dropped her hands. "Then we're right back where we started, and there's no point in discussing this further." He wheeled away from her.

Finger-combing her hair, she stood up. "I guess I'll go back to my apartment."

"Are you walking out on me? On us?"

"No. I'll never do that," she said emphatically. "I'm just tired and confused. I need to be alone, right now."

"Sure," he mumbled.

"I'd like to think that barring anything else, we'll still remain friends."

Gazing up at her sweet face, he knew his heart was hers forever, in whichever way she desired. "Always."

She hesitated, then, "Could you do me, and yourself, a favor?"

"Anything." *I'd jump off the Walt Whitman Bridge, if you asked.*

"Would you read the book of John in the Bible?"

"Sure," he said, shrugging.

"Thanks." Then she walked out.

CHAPTER THIRTY-FOUR

MONDAY MORNING BROUGHT THE INFORMATION SLADE and Stasi were waiting for. That afternoon, while Lois took Slade's car to visit some old friends in the area they sorted through the data that Arlene had faxed to Slade from her home that morning.

It had been eerie, Arlene had told Slade, but she had stayed at the office late one night last week and sifted through the personnel files. She had also gone through the desks of her fellow secretaries to glean any information they kept on hand for running personal errands for their administrators.

Sitting at her desk and studying the paperwork, Stasi was glad she didn't have to look Slade in the eye too often. It was awkward, but she was determined to stick to business. It seemed he was, too, never bringing up the subject of the night before.

Surprised at Arlene's thoroughness, Stasi said, "Arlene's wonderful, Slade. She's thought of everything."

"She certainly is wonderful. The best secretary I've ever had."

"I have an idea." She placed the papers on her desk and finally turned fully to Slade. "There's this private investigator, Steve Devlin, that I sometimes have to use for certain cases I work on. If I give him the personal information Arlene's provided us with on the partners and associate, we'd find out a lot more than if I went through the process *I* use."

Slade thought about it for a second. "How long will it take?"

"Two or three weeks."

"That long?"

"When he does a bank search, he usually has to do it for only one person. But this . . ." She gestured to the papers that contained personal information on an entire group.

"Stasi, can't *you* do it? I don't know if I can trust a stranger. I really don't like doing it at all. I've known these men for a long time, and they may not be guilty of anything."

"No, Slade, I can't do it, at least not legally. Only private investigators are authorized for it to be used as evidence in court."

He sighed resignedly. "Okay, we might as well go for it."

"Good. I'll call Steve."

Sometime after dinner, Slade called it a night and left Stasi's apartment. He looked like she felt—despondent.

Stasi visited with Lois in the living room afterward, but neither her heart nor her mind was into the light conversation.

"Stasi, honey, what's wrong between you and Slade?"

Trying to evade the question, she couldn't look Lois in the eye. "What do you mean?"

"I think you know what I mean, but if you want me to spell it out, I will. You've both lost your effervescence and try to avoid talking to or even looking at each other."

Stasi sighed heavily, picked up a lock of hair, and began winding it around her finger. "Oh, Lois, Slade wants us to have a real relationship."

"But that's good. Isn't it?"

"No. He doesn't want any strings."

"Oh. That's bad."

"He thinks he's not man enough to offer more than that."

"That's bad, too."

"I think I convinced him that his physical disability didn't matter to me."

"Oh, that's good."

"But then he brought up my faith, and his lack of."

"Mmm."

"He offered to try, though. He said he'd go to church with me, read the Bible, pray."

"Oh, good!" Lois clasped her hands to her chest.

"Well, no. I told him if he wasn't doing it for himself instead of for me, he really wasn't saved."

"True."

"So, we're still stuck in the same place as before."

"Stasi, honey, that's not so," Lois said, reaching for her hand.

"It's not?"

"Don't you see? We never know how God is working in our lives or the lives of others. It could all be a part of His plan."

Stasi nodded. "I suppose so."

"So, *I* say, let Slade go to church with you and all those other things. Being exposed to God's Word and His way could never hurt. Having a head knowledge may lead to a heart knowledge."

Stasi brightened. "You're right, Lois! I never thought of it that way." She reached over and hugged the older woman. "Thank you."

Lois returned Stasi's hug and patted her back. "Oh, honey, you're good for Slade. I'd like nothing better than to see the two of you get together."

When Stasi woke early on Tuesday morning, the cheerful sun shone gently through her bedroom window, a mirror to her mood. She'd slept well, and her heart felt light. Today she would tell Slade that she'd take him up on his offer.

But as much as she yearned to see Slade, it would have to wait. She had fallen way behind in her work, and there was a report she had promised to a client this afternoon. So she would break for lunch, spend it with Slade, and they'd talk. Rushing in with her news first thing, then hurrying off to do her work would not have been a good plan.

Time lagged on, and it was difficult for Stasi to concentrate. Though Lois was quiet as she moved about the kitchen, every little sound seemed cacophonous.

The older woman tapped her shoulder. "Sorry to disturb you, dear, but I'm going to visit with Slade while you're working."

"Okay, Lois. See you later."

"What time will you be there?"

Stasi glanced at the clock on the wall above the computer. "I'll be finished here shortly, then I'll take lunch over around noon."

"Okay." She kissed Stasi's cheek. "I'll be back before then and I won't say a word to him."

"Thanks, Lois."

After completing the report, Stasi showered and dressed in her best jeans and a cozy fleece top. In the kitchen, she prepared a salad, scooped enough for herself and Slade into a plastic container, and headed for the door.

Lois bounded through the door, just then. "I don't know if this is a good time to talk to Slade. He's expecting a visitor any minute."

"Really? Did he say who?"

"No. He evaded my questions, so I just left it alone."

"I've got to try, Lois. This may be my last chance. Hopefully, his visitor will be late." She rushed across the hall.

Outside Slade's door, Stasi took a deep breath to compose herself. Opening the door, she strode through. "Slade?" By this time, she had moved enough into the living room to glimpse Slade seated at the table in the dining area. "I made a salad," she continued, coming into full view of the entire table. She stopped, jaw dropping at the scene before her: Sitting at the table across from Slade, removing Chinese food cartons from a paper bag, was Melissa.

"I . . . I'm sorry . . ." Stasi stammered. "I didn't know . . . I didn't mean to . . ."

"Stasi," Slade began, guilt written all over his face.

"Sorry to interrupt. I . . . I'll come back later." She turned and hurried from the apartment. The last thing she heard as she rushed out the door was Slade calling for her to come back.

Slade restrained himself from chasing after her. He couldn't just leave Melissa while he followed after Stasi to profess his undying love. Besides, maybe it was wise to let it be for a while. He felt tortured by her being so close and yet so far out of his reach, and he had no guarantees about their relationship.

That decided, he sat back and relaxed while he listened to what Melissa had to say. But there was to be no end to the interruptions. A few minutes after Stasi left, Slade heard his apartment door slam and then his mother's angry voice. She must have seen how upset Stasi had been.

"Slade! What. . . oh." As she came into full view of the dining area, she stopped dead when she saw Melissa and sputtered, "I. . . I'll come back later," then turned back toward the door.

"Wait, Mom." She stopped in her tracks and turned back. "This is Melissa Kilpatrick. Melissa, this is my mother, Lois."

Lois's face registered brief recognition of the name as she walked over to the table and offered her hand to Melissa. "Hello, Melissa."

"I'm pleased to meet you, Mrs. Mitchell," Melissa replied, her cool tone belying her words.

"Just call me Lois."

"What was it you wanted, Mom?" Slade asked, impaling her with a look that dared her to actually answer.

"Oh, uh, it can wait. I'll leave you two alone." She looked at Melissa. "It was nice meeting you, Melissa." Lois hurried out of the apartment.

"This place is like a circus, the way people just walk in unannounced," Melissa complained. "You should really start locking your door, Slade."

"It's okay, I don't mind. Besides, that *was* my mother, Melissa."

"Never mind that now." The icicles dropped from her eyes, and she gazed at Slade with a familiar longing. "I've missed you."

"You have?" he asked, with raised eyebrows.

"Yes. I'm going crazy without you."

"Uh-huh," he said nonchalantly.

"You *could* show a little enthusiasm."

Slade took a bite of egg roll. "I could."

"But?"

He looked up from his meal. "Look, Melissa, what you did to me really hurt. Do you expect me to just welcome you back with open arms?"

She had the grace to look remorseful as she pushed vegetable fried rice around her plate. "What else do you want me to say?"

"'I'm sorry' would be a good start."

"I *am* sorry." Leaving her chair, she went to stand behind him, encircling his neck with her arms. "You know I am. I wouldn't be here if I weren't."

There was a time when her nearness drove him crazy, but now he felt like flinging her arms off him.

Melissa must have felt him stiffen at her touch. Straightening up, she went back to her seat and pushed more food around her plate. "You'll never give me another chance, will you?"

He thought for a moment. It seemed his relationship with Stasi was at a standstill, with no chance of moving forward. Maybe he should leave his options open. At least Melissa had never let faith come between them.

"Well?" Her green eyes were full of hope.

"Never say never." Maybe if he focused on what they used to have, his old feelings would return. "I need some time to think about it. Sort through my feelings."

"At this point, what more could I hope for?" She glanced at her watch. "I have to get back to work. Will you call me?" she asked as she slipped into her suede coat.

"Yes."

"Good." Bending down, she pressed her deep-red lipsticked lips to his, then glided out of the apartment.

As he watched her go, he realized that her kiss did nothing to stir up his emotions. Not the way Stasi's did.

Barely realizing that he was swiping the back of his hand across his mouth, he was thinking that he had to stop doing this to himself—torturing himself with thoughts of Stasi. Two days ago, she made it crystal clear that there could be no future for them if he wasn't "saved." As much as she tried to explain what that meant, he just couldn't fathom it. It all seemed ludicrous to him. Yet his mother believed in it. But if he couldn't understand any of it, how could he ever be saved?

Then he recalled Stasi's request before leaving the other day. The book of John. He promised her he'd read it. The Bible had been lying on his night table, untouched, for months. He rolled into the bedroom and over to it. Picking it up, he opened it and found the index. Leafing through to the book of John, he began reading.

CHAPTER THIRTY-FIVE

AFTER BARGING INTO HIS APARTMENT YESTERDAY, STASI hadn't seen or spoken to Slade for the remainder of the day. She knew Lois had, but she was too polite to ask what transpired between them.

The gray morning matched her mood while she unhappily sat at her computer without getting much work done. Lois had taken Slade's car to do some shopping, so Stasi didn't even have the pleasure of her company to help keep her mind off her troubles.

Close to noon, Stasi heard the door to her apartment open and Slade's voice call out.

"I'll be right out," she yelled from the bathroom. She had been trying without much success to cover up the circles and puffiness beneath her eyes using make-up and a concealer. Maybe he wouldn't notice. Sighing resignedly at herself in the mirror, she left the bathroom.

"Hi," she said, almost shyly when she entered the living room.

"Hi," he answered.

The air was thick with tension, and they sat in uncomfortable silence, eyes averted from each other, groping desperately for something to say.

"Are you all right?" Slade was the first to speak.

She looked over at him. "I feel fine. Why?"

"You don't look so well. Your eyes are sort of puffy, and you have dark circles."

Looking away again, she thought: *So much for "concealer."* "Yeah, well, I'm okay," she mumbled.

"Look, Stasi. I'm sorry you had to find Melissa at my place the way you did yesterday."

"You could have told me she was coming. I wouldn't have made a fool of myself by barging in on you."

"I only found out she was coming about an hour before."

"Why didn't you tell your mother to tell me?"

Looking down at his Nikes on the footrests of the wheelchair, he said in a low voice, "To tell you the truth, I was still sort of hurt and angry after our discussion of the day before."

She shrugged and leaned back against the sofa cushions. "So, what did Melissa want?" she asked, knowing there could be only one answer.

Clearing his throat, Slade said, "She wants to get back together."

Nodding, she turned to stare at the lamp on the table beside the couch. "What did you tell her?"

"That I had to think about it."

Staring at him searchingly, she asked, "And have you?"

"Some, but I've come to no conclusion yet."

So he *was* considering it. Where did that leave her?

"My mother told me you came over to tell me something important yesterday. What was it?" His voice sliced through her thoughts.

Sighing, she stood up and paced a bit. "I came to tell you that I'd like to offer a compromise on the offer you made me."

Raising his eyebrows, he said, "Go on."

"Well, we could go to church together, as you suggested. Praying and reading the Bible would be up to you, but we could sometimes do that together as well."

"I take it the compromise is that we wouldn't really be together?"

She stopped pacing and looked at him. "Well, we'd be *seeing* each other." She waited a beat. "As friends."

"But you'd be reaping all the benefits without a commitment. What do I get out of it?"

"Hope."

He stared at her for a moment, then bowing his head, he shook it from side to side and laughed. "This is really ironic." He looked up at her again. "Me, of all people, trying to wangle a commitment out of a woman instead of the other way around."

Stasi smiled.

Returning her smile, he shook his head again. "What have you done to me, Anastasia Courtland? I'm all upside down, inside out, and backwards."

"Good," she said, moving back to the sofa. "At least you'll never be bored with me."

He gazed at her affectionately for a moment, then propped his elbow on the armrest of the wheelchair, leaning his head into his fingertips. "I've already begun reading the Bible. The book of John, as you suggested. But you'll have to teach me how to pray."

Taken aback by his admission and his request, she quickly recovered. "No problem, but . . . what about Melissa?"

"To be honest, I'm not sure. You and I have no commitments. What if it doesn't work out? I may have to take what I can get, because I don't think there are many prospects out there for a guy like me," he finished, alluding to his condition.

"I can see your point, but I don't believe you should just 'take what you can get.'" She sighed. "Anyway, this may take some time."

His gaze was intense. "I understand that, but I hope *you* understand that I can't let it go on indefinitely."

"Understood."

"Good." A playful grin spread across his lips. "Can we seal the deal with a kiss?"

Gazing at him warily, she sighed. *Some things never change.* "All right, just one," she relented.

As she leaned toward him, grasping each armrest of the wheelchair, he gently took her face between his hands. "One *long* one," he whispered, just before his lips met hers.

Slade had been doing a lot of thinking about his future lately. He'd been out of work for months and was getting restless. The thing was, he didn't know if he felt comfortable returning to his old office. After all that had happened, the memories he had that were connected with it, he wanted to break away, get a fresh start.

He'd been toying with the idea of selling his share of the company to John or Clark, then starting all over again from scratch. Perhaps he could rent a small office right here in Haddonfield, or even work out of his apartment at first. He was sure Arlene would be more than happy to work for him.

A knock on the door plucked him from his musings. "It's open," he called.

The door opened, and John Conrad entered the apartment. "I'm taking Lois out to dinner, but I thought I'd come over and speak to you while waiting for her to finish getting ready."

Slade studied John as he walked toward him. John was tall, trim, fairly good-looking, with a trace of gray fanning out at the temples before giving way to light brown hair. Just the type of man his mother could fall for, he knew. Though he'd never met his own father, he'd seen pictures of him. Lois had been honest with him from the time he was old enough to start asking questions. Perhaps the resemblance to his father was what drew Slade to John when he was young and hoping to set the world on fire.

For some reason, he felt there was more than just a physical resemblance between the two men. Judging from what his mother had told him years ago about his father, John's attitude and person-ality were a close match. Slade worried that that was what attracted his mother to John, and he didn't want her getting hurt again. He'd always been protective of his mother, and he wasn't about to stop now.

John seated himself on the leather couch. "I thought I'd ask if you had any luck finding that disk."

"I'm sorry, John, I haven't thought about it much with all that's been going on lately." That was pretty much the truth. He had been preoccupied with this "thing" going on between him and Stasi, and also with his mother's visit.

"Do you think you could make a little time?" John asked, sounding irritated.

"Sure, John, but did you ever think I might not have the disk?"

"You must. I've torn the office apart looking for it."

There was an urgency to his tone. Why was the disk so important to him? "Is it a possibility that someone else could have gotten hold of it?" That ought to throw him a curve.

John brought a loosely fisted hand up against his mouth in apparent momentary thought. "Hmm. That idea never crossed my mind. I just assumed that since you came to me with your concerns back then, you were the one with the disk.

Slade watched John and detected a hint of desperation he'd never noticed before. He had no recollection of speaking to John concerning foul play, but now he wondered whether that was somehow connected to his so-called accident. This certainly shed a new light on his unexplained apprehensiveness toward his business partner. And now, it seemed, he had all the more reason to worry about his mother's spending time with John.

John sprung up and paced the floor. "If someone else has it, they may be waiting to somehow use it against us."

"How, and for what reason, John? Everything was brought out in the open at the time of Troy's death. There'd be no point." Unless, he thought to himself, someone else was involved in the scam.

At that moment, Lois burst through the door. "John, I'm ready. Sorry to keep you waiting."

John moved toward her and suavely raised her hand to his lips. "Not to worry, dear lady. Although it is sheer torture, you are well worth the wait."

Lois giggled and turned to Slade. "He's so gallant, isn't he?"

Trying not to show disgust, Slade forced a smile for his mother. "Oh, yeah. A regular knight in shining armor."

"We'd better go, Lois," John told her, then turning to Slade, "We'll see you later."

Slade nodded as his mother walked out the door but caught John before he followed. "Be careful with my mother, John."

The two men's eyes locked for a brief, charged moment. Slade could tell that John understood his unspoken warning and knew that it took their relationship to a whole new dimension.

CHAPTER THIRTY-SIX

PRECISELY AT NOON ON FRIDAY, DARRELL BOYD RANG Slade's doorbell. Darrell had come to pick up Slade for their prearranged lunch date. Since Stasi was working and his mother was resting, having nothing better do, Slade was ready an hour early.

Upon Slade's opening the door, the two men shook hands and greeted each other.

"Hey, Slade. How's it goin'?"

"Good, good. Everything's good, Darrell. I'm so glad to finally be getting together."

"Me too."

"I don't know about you, but I'm starving," Slade said.

"So am I. Let's go."

As they went out to the parking lot, Slade thought Darrell looked nervous. Before he hoisted himself into the passenger seat of Darrell's car, he explained how to collapse the chair. Darrell had a small problem but finally got it.

They had lunch at a tiny restaurant on Station Avenue in Haddon Heights. In spite of its size, the place had a reputation for its delicious food and quality service; hence, it was jam-packed.

Slade and Darrell were seated at a small corner table. Slade ordered an eggplant parmigiano sandwich, while Darrell had a good old-fashioned burger with all the fixings.

Slade had been observing Darrell since he picked him up, and it seemed his jitters had begun to subside.

"So how are things at the office for you?" Slade asked him.

"My workload's a little heavier," he answered, dipping a French fry in ketchup, "but I can handle it."

"I have no doubt about that."

"That aspect of it is fine, but . . . I don't know . . . there's this creepy aura in the office ever since the thing with Troy."

"Creepy in what way?" Slade took a huge bite of his sandwich.

"Oh," Darrell's eyes moved to the ceiling, then around the room, as if trying to picture scenes from a different place and time. "I don't know. Like John. He's been acting real weird."

"In what way?"

"He's been searching people's offices and desks. Especially yours. You should see it, man, it's a disaster area."

"He told me he was looking for something," Slade remarked nonchalantly.

"He's also been asking a lot of questions of everyone." He wiped his mouth with a napkin and sat back. "That's just some days. Other days he stays in his office for hours and never comes out till closing time. And still other days, he doesn't even show up!"

"That's all totally out of character for John," Slade said before sipping his soft drink.

"It sure is." Darrell's eyes were as big as golf balls.

"I'm sure things will settle down," Slade assured him. "There's been a lot going on recently." Darrell nodded in response. "After all," Slade continued, "John takes pride in the firm and is probably upset that these things could be happening."

"I guess you're right," Darrell agreed.

Darrell seemed satisfied then, and their talk turned to other subjects. Slade felt he had done a good job of convincing Darrell of the insignificance of John's behavior, but he'd done a lousy job of it on himself.

Another thing to add to his list of worries.

On Sunday, Slade and Lois attended an early church service with Stasi. They sat at the far end of the last pew so that the aisle could accommodate Slade's wheelchair.

Slade was impressed at the warmth and sincerity of the welcome he and his mother received. Many people at the sight of newcomers stopped to say hello and introduce themselves. When Slade was presented to Stasi's friend Rachel Darrow, he noticed a knowing glance pass between the two young women. Assuming he had passed inspection, he relaxed in his chair to observe the mechanics of the service.

Both surprise and relief surged through him. Visions of questionable prophecy, spurious healings, and people wailing had always come to mind at the thought of a born-again Christian church service. But this . . . it was no different from the mundane Sunday meetings in the little country churches depicted on television.

At first he became a little bored. Almost the entire first half of the service was filled with singing and pastoral prayer. When the time finally came for the sermon, though finding it a little interesting, he thought it somewhat long and was lost about halfway through.

After the service, on the way out, he caught snippets of conversation, mostly exclamations over what a great message had been preached. Even Stasi and Lois were talking about it as they left the church.

Slade felt left out. He really didn't get what was being taught, and he couldn't see the greatness of it. All he knew was that he'd have to put up with it to keep up his end of the bargain with Stasi.

CHAPTER THIRTY-SEVEN

HE SAT ALONE IN HIS OFFICE CONTEMPLATING WHAT COULD have gone wrong. The whole thing had become one big mess. Everything ran smoothly for a while—until Slade started to catch on. He couldn't fault him for that; he'd always known Slade was sharp. In fact, he admired the man's astuteness.

But not enough to let it ruin his life.

No more pussyfooting around. It was time to figure out a way to force Slade's hand. He needed a plan and thought hard for some time. Finally, it was as though a light bulb had gone on in his head. It would take some time to implement, but it would work.

Mentally devising his scheme, he prepared to leave the office. Smiling in relief, John switched off his desk lamp.

CHAPTER THIRTY-EIGHT

STASI WAS HARD AT WORK ON HER COMPUTER WHEN SLADE entered her apartment. Since Lois was meeting John for lunch, Slade had offered to make sandwiches for himself and Stasi.

They went into the kitchen, and Slade unwrapped two ham-and-cheese sandwiches while Stasi poured fruit punch into two glasses.

As they ate, Slade kept staring at Stasi, and she could see a question burning in his eyes. Finally, he spoke.

"Stasi, I'd like to ask you something."

"Okay."

"Well, the way my mother's been acting, and things she says—even looks she throws your way—they all tell me that maybe she knows about our little deal, even helped you plan it. Is that so?"

Her hand shook as she lifted her sandwich from the plate in front of her. "Yes, Slade," she replied, avoiding his eyes. "She asked me what was wrong between us, so I told her. She knows everything," she added, suddenly very interested in her sandwich.

"Did she help you plan the whole thing?"

She looked at him now and sighed. Pursing her lips, she said, "She helped me see reason. We decided that if you were willing to compromise, I should accept. It could be part of God's plan, for all we knew. And we thought, perhaps in time, you'd . . ."

"Convert?" he finished for her.

She nodded solemnly, feeling like a child caught with her hand in the cookie jar.

Slade shook his head. "Stasi, really," he admonished. "There's no need to feel so bad about it. No one can force me to do anything I don't want to do. So relax. Whatever happens, happens. I know your intentions are good."

"I know all of that." She placed the sandwich on the plate and pushed the plate back. "And, yes, my intentions *are* good, but I feel like I've been deceiving you in some way." She squeezed her eyes shut and bowed her head. "I'm sorry. It's just that I really want . . ."

Suddenly he was next to her, his arm pulling her against his chest. "I know, babe. I know. I do, too. Don't worry."

She smiled up at him in relief. "Thanks for being so understanding."

He was looking down at her, studying her face, her eyes. "You really can't stand anything that even *remotely* resembles lying, can you?"

Shaking her head, she said, "No, I can't."

"But why? I know Christians are dead set against lying, but it seems to go deeper than that with you. What is it, Stasi?"

She gently pushed away from his embrace. Should she tell him now? This *might* be a good time to let him see who she really was, or at least *had* been at one time.

"Look, I'll tell you," she said, standing and gathering the plates and glasses. "But let's get comfortable in the living room first."

"Uh-oh. Is it that bad?" Slade joked, wheeling toward the living room.

She frowned at him, then helped him onto the sofa and saw that he was comfortable. Sitting beside him, she said, "I think I've mentioned that I have an older sister, Lauren, in Virginia, whom I rarely have contact with."

Slade nodded.

"The reason we don't see or speak with each other much is that we never really got along. Then, when I was thirteen, I did something that made the situation even worse."

Her hands were shaking, and she clasped them together to steady them.

Slade waited silently, his eyes glued to her.

"Lauren was always the wild one, constantly getting into trouble. I was usually the shy, quiet one, but one day, my friend Jenny and I decided we wanted to try smoking cigarettes. Jenny stole an entire pack from her father's carton, and we hid behind the shed in our backyard to do it."

She sat forward on the couch, focusing on the distant scene. Slade gently laid a hand on her back.

"Before we got a chance to light up, my mom came out of the house, calling to us about having a snack. We were so scared; we dashed out from behind the shed, leaving the pack of cigarettes propped against the rear wall of it. Later, after Jenny left, I remembered the cigarettes, retrieved them, and ran to the room I shared with Lauren to hide them. Before I could find a good, safe spot, I heard footsteps in the hall and, in a panic, stashed them between the box spring and mattress of Lauren's bed, since it was closest to me. Lauren came into the room, but she didn't notice or suspect a thing.

"A week later, my mother was changing the bedding, and the cigarettes fell out when she pulled off the top sheet that was tucked in at the foot of the bed. When my parents confronted Lauren, she, of course, denied they were hers, but so did I. Since Lauren was always the one getting into trouble, my parents believed they were really hers and punished her severely, mostly because they thought she had lied." Sniffing back tears, Stasi hid her face in her hands. "I let them do it and never said a word!"

Slade pulled her back to rest her head against his chest. "Stasi, honey, you were only a kid."

"But I knew better. And it only made things worse between us, because Lauren knew I had to have been the one to put those cigarettes there. She never forgave me for it."

"You're kidding."

"No. But after I was born again, I admitted to her my guilt and asked her forgiveness. She accepted my apology, but we are still somewhat estranged."

"I'm sorry, Stasi." He kissed her hair.

"But immediately after that incident, I promised myself I'd never lie again."

"You paid for your mistake with your guilt. Everything's fine now."

Pulling herself up, she looked at him. "But everything's not fine. You see, I broke that promise some time ago."

"What happened?"

She laid her head against his chest again. She needed the sustenance it provided. After telling him what she was about to tell him, she wasn't sure whether she'd ever find herself in his embrace again. As if he could feel her apprehension, Slade tightened his arms around her in reassurance.

"I told you about my fiancé's death."

"Yes."

"Well, there's more to it than what I told you." When he didn't respond, she went on. "My parents were out, and I was alone, but Barry didn't really want to come over that night. He'd worked late and was tired. When I couldn't get him to change his mind, I selfishly pretended to have heard a noise outside the house so that he'd offer to come over and look around. I acted frightened, at the same time telling him not to worry, it was probably nothing, knowing he wouldn't rest until he checked everything out for me." She lifted a hand to swipe at a tear she felt running down her cheek before continuing. "It was on the way over that . . . ." She couldn't keep the tears in check, and her sobbing rang in her own ears.

"Shhh," Slade comforted, rubbing her arm. "There's no need to go on. I get it."

Pulling away from him, she covered her face with her hands. "Don't you see? It's *my* fault. *I'm* responsible for his death. And now I have to live with that knowledge for the rest of my life!" Taking a tissue from her jeans pocket, she blew her nose. "His family never forgave me. And I'll never forget the things his mother screamed at me after the funeral service."

Slade pulled her back into his arms. "Stasi, honey, listen. You have to forgive yourself and move on. I'm always hearing about how God forgives anything as long as we ask. I'm sure you know He's forgiven you. All you have to do is let it go now."

"I know, Slade. I know He's forgiven me, but it's a lot harder to forgive myself."

"Give it more time."

"I've no choice but to do that." They sat silently for a moment, then Stasi said, "I thought you'd be repulsed by what I just told you."

He chuckled softly. "Me? Of all people? Who am I to judge?" He absently smoothed her hair back from her face. "God knows I've done a lot of things to be ashamed of. I could never be the one to throw stones."

"But you've always been honest. You never pretended to be someone you're not."

"Neither do you. I've always admired that about you. You don't play games like a lot of people do."

"Except for that one time."

"Everyone makes mistakes, but it helps if we learn from them. It's clear that you have, and now you've moved on."

"Yes, but thankfully, I have the Lord to see me through the tough times. It was in my grief and sorrow that I turned to Him and was born again."

"Amen."

She knew he didn't mean that the way a believer would, but she lifted her head to look up at him and say, "You seem to be full of biblical wisdom lately. You've really been reading your Bible, haven't you?"

"I promised you I would, and I always keep my promises," he replied, placing a kiss on her forehead.

CHAPTER THIRTY-NINE

ON SATURDAY AFTERNOON SLADE WAS PUMPING IRON when Stasi burst through the door of his apartment. "Slade!"

"In here," he called from his combination home office and weight room.

"Hi," she said, rushing into the room. "I just got this in the mail." She held up a thick, business-sized envelope. "This is Steve Devlin's report on bank records of everyone we asked him to check on at Conrad, Mitchell. I haven't opened it yet."

"Let's take a look at it. Go ahead and open it."

Stasi sat in the chair at the desk, and Slade wheeled himself close by. Taking a metal opener from the top drawer, Stasi slit the top of the envelope and removed the wad of papers. She unfolded the stack and straightened them by bending the sections backward at the fold line. Laying them flat on the desk, she began to study them, handing Slade each page as she went through them.

The room was silent for some time except for the occasional soft sound of paper rustling as they went through each page of the report.

Everything was in it: multiple bank accounts, huge sums of money. And every partner except Slade seemed to be involved, nor was Darrell Boyd involved.

Giving Slade time to finish the last page, Stasi asked, "Well? What do you think?"

He blew out a long, tortured sigh. "I think your friend, Steve Devlin, is very good at what he does."

She frowned at him. "Forget that! What do you think of the information in his report?"

Slowly, Slade placed the report on the desk, then spun the chair around and rolled over to the one window in the room and stared out through the open blinds. Long, silent moments ticked by before he answered. "Frankly, Stasi, I'm stunned. I don't know what to think, what to say."

Stasi remained quiet.

Suddenly the enormity of the situation hit Slade full in the face, and his anger erupted with volcanic force. "What an idiot I am!" he yelled, slamming his fist on the armrest of the wheelchair. "They must all be laughing at me behind my back! Everyone I thought I could trust has been playing me for a fool. Every single one." He separately ground out the words, ending the last on a high, anxious note.

Stasi's arms coiled around his neck from behind, and he felt her cheek against the top of his head. He immediately drew strength from her comforting embrace. She was his rock, the one sure thing he could count on at the moment. He wondered whether he could ever go on without her.

Something else to think about. He brought his hands up and clasped the soft smaller ones that were joined together just below his neck. He was in love with this woman. She was his mainstay. A constant through all his troubles. But all of that had to be set aside for the moment. Later, he would pick it apart piece by piece and examine each of those pieces very closely before making any decisions.

"It doesn't really mean anything," she said quietly. "There could be dozens of reasons for it."

"Name one."

Silence. Finally, she said. "Okay, I can't think of anything offhand, but let's not jump to conclusions."

Lifting his hand to rub his forehead, he emitted a weary sigh. "Right. I suppose we should be very careful before we point any fingers."

She moved away from him now, and he felt as though a part of him went with her.

"Yes. Let's take our time, think it through very carefully."

He turned from the window to see her moving toward the door. "You're leaving?"

"I have some errands. I'll pick up a pizza on the way home. Will Lois be here for dinner?"

"I think so. But Stasi, let's not bring this up in front of her until we're sure what to do. She still doesn't know that this," he inclined his head toward his body, indicating its condition, "was no accident." He still cringed at the thought of applying the words *murder* and *kill* in reference to his circumstances.

"Sure thing, Slade. I had every intention of letting you decide when to tell her about it. But keep in mind that it will have to be soon. We're not sure if it's safe for her to be seeing John now that we know what we know. See you later." She gracefully slipped through the door and was gone.

He had a lot of things to think about. Could all of his colleagues have been involved in one big scam without his knowledge? All except Darrell Boyd? Would he himself also be implicated in the end?

It was too much to handle at the moment. He'd wait for Stasi, and they'd figure it out together. They made a great team. Which brought him back to earlier thoughts.

His love for Stasi.

He knew she had *some* feelings for him, because although she was the kind of person to have love and compassion for all humankind, she was not a woman who played games with a man's heart.

But what did he have to offer her? She was a vivacious young woman who did not deserve to be shackled to an invalid for the rest of her life. Of course she was noble about it, saying it didn't matter to her. But it mattered to *him*. The very thought of being dependent upon someone, especially a woman, for the rest of his life turned his stomach. Sure, he depended on her now for many things, but it would be different to expect a life-long commitment to such a burden.

Then why was he bothering with their bargain? He was confused, feeling like the rope in a tug-of-war. On the one hand, he wanted to be a part of her life, wanted a commitment from her. On the other hand, he cared for her too much to really expect that from her. She deserved better.

What was wrong with him? He had never been so indecisive in his life.

Dear Lord, help me to be strong in my decision.

His body snapped to attention at this unintended plea. Since when had he started praying?

CHAPTER FORTY

JOHN CONRAD HAD INVITED LOIS TO SEE HIS CABIN IN THE Pocono Mountains on Sunday. They left immediately after the church service, and he had told her that they would be back late but that they could make the trip both ways in a day.

She hadn't had a chance to tell Slade or Stasi about the trip. When John dropped her off the night before, Stasi was at Slade's apartment. She had been too tired to wait up and, not wanting to disturb them, decided she would tell them in the morning. Only she hadn't had a chance in the morning, either. They all overslept and rushed like mad to get to church on time. On the way home, there was so much playful banter between Stasi and Slade that she completely forgot about telling them. While Stasi helped Slade get settled in at his apartment, Lois barely had time to change clothes before John appeared to pick her up. He seemed to be in a hurry, but she made him wait while she scribbled a brief note of explanation.

The anxiety of rushing around and not having the opportunity to apprise the young people of her sojourn with John took its toll. The chest pains were beginning. Lois told John to go on down to the car and she would be there momentarily. Instead, John squawked and waited by the door as Lois quickly placed a nitroglycerin tablet under her tongue. In her haste, she left the vial of remaining pills on the counter next to the sink before rushing out the door with John.

More than a little uncomfortable at the idea of being with John all those hours, she squirmed in the passenger seat of John's Mercedes, as she had done in the pew during the sermon. Moreover, as a result of the extensive amount of time she had spent with John, it appeared to others that her fondness for him went far beyond what she actually felt. But because Slade and Stasi had some issues to iron out, she wanted to give them as much time to themselves as possible.

That's not to say that she didn't enjoy herself when in John's company, for he took her to the best places and was always a gentleman. But the best thing about it was that it gave her an opportunity to present the gospel to him. John would scoff and change the subject when she brought it up, but at least she was planting the seed . . .

What bothered Lois most about the whole thing was that in spite of all the politeness and charm he exhibited, John seemed to have an underlying sinister quality that gave her the creeps.

Now, in the confines of his car, Lois turned and smiled tentatively at John. He returned that smile in a seemingly smug manner as they sped along the Skuylkill Expressway toward the Poconos.

CHAPTER FORTY-ONE

WHEN STASI RETURNED TO HER APARTMENT AFTER HELPING Slade get settled, she found Lois's note on the kitchen counter. Slade wasn't going to like this.

Hurrying across the hall, she burst through Slade's door. "Slade!"

"In the kitchen!"

Rounding the corner, she said, "Lois has gone off with John."

"Gone off? What do you mean, gone off?" he asked, sounding anxious.

Handing him Lois's note, she said, "Look."

Quickly scanning the note, he breathed out a tremulous sigh. "The Poconos. He's taken her to the mountains!" he yelled, breathing heavily.

"Let's not jump to any conclusions, Slade," Stasi advised, stepping aside as he rolled past her out of the kitchen. "Maybe he really does only want to show her his cabin. They'll probably be back sometime tonight."

Stopping in the living room, he whirled the chair around. "I can't take that chance!" he boomed up at her.

Lowering her head, she stared down at the carpet. He hadn't raised his voice to her since he was in the hospital. She knew he was anguished, but she was only trying to be helpful.

He wheeled over to her, took her hand, and led her to the sofa. "Sit down," he said quietly, still holding her hand. "I'm sorry, honey. I'm just worried about my mom, and I can't seem to trust anyone like I used to." He brought her hand up and kissed it. "Except you."

She smiled tremulously. "That's okay, Slade. I understand."

He smiled back and winked. "Good." Letting go of Stasi's hand, he leaned back in the wheelchair and sighed. "We should have told her everything before this."

"Maybe, but we didn't, so let's just deal with it the best we can."

He nodded.

"Now," she said, rising, "I think we should show Steve's report to Detective Jessup. Just so he's aware."

"Okay, you're probably right."

"We'll stop along the way and have a copy made to give to him."

"Sure."

An hour later, they arrived at the Williamstown Police Station. Jessup wasn't in, so they left the report on his desk with an explanatory note that included the fact that John had whisked Lois away to the mountains.

Returning home, they had nothing to do but wait. They whiled away the time playing Scrabble after eating an early dinner and watching television.

By ten-thirty Stasi's eyes were drooping, and she told Slade she was going to turn in.

"Okay, but will you leave a note for my mom to either poke her head in or call over to let me know when she gets home? I don't think I'll be able to sleep until I know she's back."

"Sure," she said, bending down to kiss his forehead.

Before she could move away, he reached up, cupped her face with his hands, and brought her lips down to his. "What would I do without you?" he asked when he broke the kiss.

He had a look in his eyes that she hadn't seen before that rendered her speechless. Giving his hand a quick squeeze, she simply smiled and left.

Slade had been stretched out on the sofa reading his Bible when the phone rang. Startled, he glanced at his watch. Twelve-fifteen. Probably his mom calling to tell him she arrived home. He reached for the cordless phone he had purposely left lying on the nearby coffee table.

"Hello?" he answered it, feeling relieved.

"Slade?"

The relief was quickly squelched when he realized it wasn't his mother, but he recognized the voice. His heart began racing. "John?"

"Yes."

John's voice sounded strange, and Slade didn't like it. Slade's palms became moist, and the hair on the back of his neck stood on end. "What is it, John? Is my mother still with you? Is she okay?"

"Yes, Slade, she's with me, and she's okay. For now."

"What do you mean?" He struggled into a sitting position.

"You have something I want. Bring it to me, and Lois goes free. If not. . . well, you don't want to think about what will happen to her."

"But what do I have that you could possibly want?"

"Think for a moment, Slade. You'll figure it out. I always admired your astuteness. It was one of the reasons I took you under my wing."

"I don't know what you're talking about. What . . ." Then he remembered. "The disk?"

"Bingo."

"But why?"

"I think you can figure that out, too. But that can wait. Bring the disk to my cabin in the Poconos. Quickly."

"I want to talk to my mother first."

"I'm afraid that isn't possible. You see she's, uh . . . indisposed."

"What do you mean? What have you done to her?" he yelled into the phone.

He heard a low chuckle from John's end. "Now, now, son, calm down. Don't worry, she'll be fine. I put something in her hot chocolate to make her sleep. She'll probably be out until morning."

"You listen to me, John. My mother has a heart condition, and if anything happens to her, I'll personally tear you from limb to limb."

His soft, sinister laugh trickled through the phone line. "You? How do you propose to do that from a wheelchair?"

"Trust me. I can do it." He sounded surer than he felt.

This time, John emitted a loud laugh. "I believe that you can, Slade. If by no other means than sheer will."

Slade decided he'd had enough of the verbal swordplay, and he was running out of patience. "Tell me where your cabin is."

"You mean you don't remember?" he asked with what Slade felt was a mix of mock surprise and sympathy.

"No."

"Ah, your lack of memory," John taunted. He rattled off directions while Slade struggled to write them down. Then in a deadly serious tone, he added, "You are to come alone. No police, though I realize you'll need Stasi to drive you up. But that's it. If you try anything funny you'll never see your mother again." He hung up.

Slade slammed the phone into the sofa cushions. He needed a plan. One thing was for sure: There was no way John was getting that disk. It would be like signing his own death warrant, as well as his mother's.

Hiking himself from the sofa and into his wheelchair, Slade sped out of the apartment and over to Stasi's. He rang the doorbell and pounded on the door simultaneously. "Stasi! Wake up!" he repeated over and over for what seemed to him hours but in reality was only minutes.

Barely able to contain his impatience while listening to the slide of the deadbolt and the rattle of the doorknob, he shot through the door as soon as it was opened, nearly running Stasi over.

"Slade!" she shrieked, rubbing the sleep from her eyes. "What is it?"

"I just got a call from John."

"What is it? Has something happened to Lois?"

"Yeah! What's happened is he's kidnapped her."

Incredulous, she moved toward the couch and dropped herself on it. Closing her eyes, she shook her head. Then it seemed a thought struck her as she quickly raised her eyes to Slade. "He wants the disk?"

He nodded. "You got it, baby."

"What should we do?"

There it was again. "We." She included herself as if she were a natural part of every circumstance in his life. And he loved her all the more for it.

"I know I can't let John have that disk. If he ever got hold of it, we'd all be sitting ducks. We have to figure out how to get my mom back without giving it to him."

Stasi rose from the couch. "We'll need clear heads. I'll make us some coffee while we work it through." She went to the kitchen and measured coffee into the filter while Slade pulled his chair up to the table.

Stasi took a seat across from Slade while they waited for the coffee to brew. "Should we call Detective Jessup?"

"No!" he shot at her emphatically. "He said we're to go alone or he'll kill her."

"But Slade, what do you think he intends to do once we get there and he gets the disk? Do you think he'll let us all just walk out the door?"

"No. As I said, I don't want to give him the disk, but I need a backup plan."

They sat at the table, drinking coffee and mulling it over for forty-five minutes before coming up with something feasible. They needed a second copy of the disk and the address and directions to John's cabin, then a visit to Darrell Boyd.

Stasi left the table to throw on some clothes while Slade cleared the coffee mugs from the table. Putting the mugs in the sink, he reached for the faucet to run water in them when he spotted a pill vial at the back of the counter. He knew what it was before he even picked it up. It belonged to his mother. Her heart medication. His hand trembled as he read the label. "No!" he screamed in his head over and over before he realized he was yelling it aloud.

Stasi rushed out from the bedroom. "Slade, what's the matter?" He silently held the pill vial out to her. She took it and read the label, then gasped. "Her heart medicine! I found it beside the sink and just pushed it back without giving it a thought." She slipped it into her jeans pocket. "We'll take it with us just in case."

They rushed to Slade's apartment. He took out the disk and slipped it into his computer to copy. While Stasi wrote down the address and directions to John's cabin, along with Jessup's phone number, Slade dialed Darrell Boyd's number.

A sleepy voice answered on the third ring. "Hello?"

"Darrell?"

"Yeah, this is Darrell. Who's this?"

"It's Slade."

"Man, it's one-fifteen in the morning!"

"I know, and I'm sorry about that, but I need your help. It's a matter of life or death."

Darrell was immediately contrite. "Sure, what can I do?"

Before giving him instructions, Slade explained in an abbreviated version everything that had transpired, from the skydiving incident to his mother's kidnapping by John.

Darrell emitted a low whistle. "I can't believe it. And neither one of us knew it."

"No. It was going on right under our noses the whole time."

"Okay, just tell me what you need, buddy."

Slade hesitated for a moment. "I need to drop some things off to you. Is that okay? I know it's late."

"That's fine. I'll be waiting."

When Slade and Stasi arrived at Darrell's house, they found his wife, Lavon, had been waiting up with him. She expressed her concern and offered to pray for them. Slade shot her a curious glance before responding. "Thank you, Lavon. We could sure use your prayers."

Slade gave Darrell the disk along with Stasi's written notes and specific verbal instructions as to what to do should he not hear from Slade by five that morning. Before leaving, he turned his wheelchair to face Darrell. Gripping Darrell's hand in a farewell handshake, Slade said, "When this is all over, I'd like you and me to talk about forming a new partnership."

Darrell's eyes widened and lit up. "Sure, Slade. I'd like that. Be careful out there, buddy."

Then Slade and Stasi left the house and headed for the mountains.

CHAPTER FORTY-TWO

THE EXPRESSWAY WAS DEVOID OF TRAFFIC AND STRETCHED before them like an endless ribbon of licorice. Slade and Stasi remained quiet for most of the trip, both lost in their own thoughts. When Slade finally spoke, Stasi was suddenly jolted from the mesmerism of the velvety black road ahead.

"I'm going to check my answering machine in case John called," he said, pulling a cell phone from his jacket pocket.

"Good idea."

Slade seemed to be taking a long time listening to messages, and Stasi glanced at him a couple of times. Finally, Slade cut the call, then began punching in a number.

"Did he call?"

Slade nodded and kept punching numbers, his lips moving slightly as if trying not to lose a number he'd memorized a second ago.

"What did he say?" she asked after he punched the last button.

Holding the phone to his ear, he answered, "He said we're taking too long, we'd better be on our way, then left his number."

Before Stasi had a chance to respond, Slade turned his attention to the call, and she listened.

"John? Slade. We're on our way." Silence as he listened to John on the other end. "About halfway there. Right." He clicked off and deposited the phone back into his pocket.

"That was short and sweet," Stasi said.

"Believe me, I don't want to talk to that man any more than I have to."

"But what will you say when we get there?"

"I haven't a clue." He paused for a few seconds, then, "Stasi?"

"Hmm?"

"Could . . . could we pray before we get there?"

Shocked, she turned to look at him. "Sure." Pulling onto the shoulder of the road, she turned off the ignition and faced him. "Okay, ready?"

"Yes," he answered, "but I'll lead the prayer this time. I have some things I want to say."

His gaze held a special meaning, but she dared not let her mind form the wish that had been buried deep in her heart for many months. She just managed to shake her head and bow it.

As she listened to Slade pour out his heart to the Lord, she could barely contain herself. She wanted to leap from the seat and shout for joy. Her heart was doing a jig in her chest, and she wanted to join in, for her most fervent prayer had finally been answered. Slade was committing his life to Jesus Christ! How she wished she could attend the party that was going on in heaven right now!

She forced herself to settle down, however, because now Slade was praying for his mother's safety and for God to provide them with the strength and ability to save her.

The prayer ended, and Stasi peered at Slade through a blur of tears.

"Well, say something," he prodded.

Speechless, she just smiled and shook her head, but she knew he could tell she was happy.

There was so much she *did* want to say, but now was not the time. And time was something they were running out of.

Starting up the car again, she pulled onto the highway.

CHAPTER FORTY-THREE

SLADE THOUGHT THE CABIN LOOKED FRIENDLY AND INVITING when Stasi pulled the car into the driveway. Lights blazed from the windows and the front porch. The whole thing seemed surreal, he thought as he pulled himself into the wheelchair Stasi unfolded before him.

They approached the front entrance, and Stasi instructed Slade to wait at the bottom of the steps while she asked John for help.

Stasi raised the brass door knocker and banged it three times. John immediately pulled open the door. "It's about time you got here!" he snapped.

Stasi looked surprised and took a small step back. She probably hadn't expected to have her head bitten off.

"What did you expect?" she countered. "It's not as though you're in the next town."

"Where's Slade?"

"Down there." John saw her gesture in the direction where Slade waited. "I need help getting him up the steps."

"What?" He walked through the door to the edge of the porch and glared down the four steps at Slade. "Oh. Of course."

John took the handles, and Stasi took the footrims. Together they lifted the chair up the four steps.

Slade hated it. The feeling of dependency, inadequacy. It was all downright embarrassing. He had come here to rescue his mother, and the villain had to help him into the house!

He had to remember that he was to give up *himself* and his own selfish desires and let God work through him.

Closing his eyes, Slade took a deep, cleansing breath. *Okay, I'm ready.*

They all went into the cabin, which brought them directly into a spacious but cozy living room. In any other circumstances, the overstuffed sofa positioned before the fireplace would beckon to him invitingly. This was a scene of peacefulness.

He felt anything *but* peace at the moment. "Where's my mother?" was the first thing Slade blurted.

"She's in another part of the house, but don't worry, she's safe."

"I need to see her. She may need her medication."

"That'll have to wait. First things first," John spat. "Now, where's the disk?"

"I have it right here." Slade pulled a disk from his jacket pocket and handed it to John.

John examined the disk, then walked to the far end of the room where a Cherry wood desk bore a computer. He slipped the disk into the drive and punched some keys.

Seemingly satisfied, he turned to Slade. "I'm glad you weren't stupid enough to hand over a bogus disk."

"I knew you'd be too smart to fall for a stunt like that."

"Smart man."

Slade rolled closer to John. "Where's my mother?"

"She's asleep upstairs in one of the bedrooms. I put enough sleeping pills in her hot chocolate to knock her out for some time," John explained as he reached into the inside breast pocket of his expensive suit. "But there's no reason to disturb her now," he said as he pulled out a small handgun and pointed it at Slade.

Slade heard Stasi's sharp intake of breath, but he was not surprised at John's underhandedness, and he knew his face reflected that fact. Stasi had come up to stand beside him, and he instinctively pushed her behind his wheelchair in a protective gesture.

"You can't protect her, Slade, or your mother."

Slade narrowed his eyes at John. "I'm capable of more than you think."

"I'm not talking about your capabilities." John waved the gun around in gesturing with his hands as he spoke. "I don't want to use this, but I will if I need to. So if you don't want me to, you'll both do exactly as I tell you."

Slade felt Stasi rest her hand tenderly on his shoulder, and he reached up and grasped it. "What makes you think we'll make it so easy for you?" Slade asked John.

"Because if you don't, I'll shoot you. All of you." He gestured with the gun. "Now get on that sofa."

Slade could see that they had no other choice at the moment. He still hadn't played his trump card, but he would save it for later. They needed to stall for time.

"Okay, John, but first I'd like to ask you something."

John studied him a few seconds before responding. "I guess I can allow you that much, though I don't promise I'll answer."

"What I want to know is, why? Why did you get caught up in all this in the first place?"

"That's a long story." He moved to perch himself on the edge of the desk. "You see, I was already caught up in it before you even knew me."

Slade stared at him. "I don't believe it."

"It's true. It started with my first two divorces. I worked hard and brought in lots of money, but I had to split everything evenly with each wife. But I wanted more, felt I deserved more, especially since *I* was the breadwinner. That's when I put together my little scheme. It still wasn't enough. I needed help, and I started looking around for a young man with the same drive and determination I had. That's when you came on the scene."

Slade covered his eyes with one hand and shook his head. "I was helping you cheat, and I wasn't even aware of it."

Pushing away from the desk, John paced in the small area where he was standing. "Oh, but you weren't."

Surprised, Slade raised his head and looked at John questioningly.

"That's right. You see, when I learned of your background— where you grew up, that you were a member of various gangs at various times, your financial circumstances—I thought you'd be determined to collect what the world owed you—any way that you could."

"Never," Slade mumbled.

John stopped pacing. "That's exactly what I found out. But by that time, it was too late. You were already a partner, and since you were bringing in a large portion of the profits, I felt it didn't matter, and I began looking around for someone else."

"Troy."

"Yes. After that, it grew into a huge operation that kept everybody happy. Until you stuck your nose into it. Now, because of you, Troy is dead and I have to leave the country."

"What about Clark?"

"He can do as he pleases. He was in on the scam but not the attempt on your life. Thankfully, Troy was loyal to me on that count." For a second, his features took on a sorrowful expression.

Slade glared at John, shaking his head. "Everything I know I learned from you. You were my mentor, my friend, the father I never had." For the second time in his adult life, he wanted to cry. He had placed all of his hope and trust into a fake. "Until now, I always counted you among the best."

"Sorry to disappoint you, son, but we all do what we have to do." His expression suddenly changed. "Now stop stalling and get on that sofa!" he snapped.

It was time to tell him. "John, it's only fair to warn you that I gave a copy of the disk to Darrell Boyd with the address to this cabin and instructions to call the police if he doesn't hear from me in," he glanced at his watch, "half an hour."

John looked at Slade. His eyes were half angry, half admiring. "Well. You've thought of everything. I'll just have to act more quickly, won't I?" He pointed the gun in the direction of the sofa. "Now get over there!"

They had no choice but to comply.

A small table in the corner of the room held a tray of liquor and soda bottles, along with an ice bucket. John went over to it and poured ginger ale into two glasses. He removed a pill vial from a side pocket of his suit jacket, extracted a handful of pills from it, and dropped half of them into each glass. Swishing the liquid around, he placed the glasses on a small serving tray. Holding the gun in one hand and balancing the tray in the other, he approached Slade and Stasi, offering each of them the soda.

CHAPTER FORTY-FOUR

DARRELL SAT AT THE KITCHEN TABLE, SIPPING COFFEE and glancing at the clock every few minutes, as if that were to make the hands move faster. After Slade and Stasi left, he had told Lavon to go back to bed. She was reluctant at first, but suddenly drowsy, she finally went. He almost wished he hadn't made her go. It would have been comforting to have her sitting beside him at this moment, offering solace and reassurance, sharing his coffee.

He glanced at the clock again. Forty-five minutes to go before Slade told him to call the police. It felt like he'd been sitting here forever. He stared at the phone on the table beside him, willing it to ring. No go.

He was apprehensive. Suppose he waited, as Slade told him he should do? It could be too late by then. Maybe he should call now. Forty-five minutes might not make too much of a difference. No. He'd better wait and do as Slade said. But suppose there was a reason he hadn't yet called?

He quickly picked up the phone and began punching in the numbers.

CHAPTER FORTY-FIVE

LOIS WOKE SLOWLY, HER MIND FUZZY. THERE WAS A dim light on. Sitting up, she looked around the room, not recognizing it.

Puzzled, she searched her memory. The last thing she recalled was sitting in front of a cozy fire with John, sipping hot chocolate.

What time was it? Day or night? She pulled aside the heavy curtains covering the window and peered out. It was dark out, but the sky wasn't black. Sort of a dark, deep blue, indicating the approaching dawn.

She couldn't figure it out. What had happened? Had she passed out? Fallen asleep without realizing it?

By now she realized she must still be at John's cabin in the mountains and was sure that Slade and Stasi were beside themselves with worry.

Hurrying to the door, she intended to pull it hard, but something told her to ease it open quietly. If John were asleep, she wouldn't want to wake him. She would just find a phone to call her son and tell him where she was.

Grasping the knob, she gently turned it all the way to the left, then slowly pulled the door toward her. What a shock she received when, upon opening the door a crack, a chain appeared across her line of vision! *Why on earth would there be a chain on the* outside *of a bedroom door? And why am I locked in?*

Gradually, Lois became aware of voices coming from downstairs. Opening the door as wide as the chain would allow, she peered through the crack and spotted a railing across the landing. Lois stood quietly, listening to the voices and trying to make out what they were saying. John's voice was instantly recognizable, but the other two voices were lower, muffled at first. She could definitely tell that one of the voices was female. Then the man's voice rose slightly in timbre, and she immediately recognized it, though she was astounded as to why her son would be there.

Calming herself, she rationalized that he had come to take her home. Perhaps John had called him. It occurred to her that the woman, of course, would be Stasi. She would have to have driven Slade up.

About to call out, she stopped herself. It sounded as though a commotion had erupted, and she wasn't sure anyone would hear her. Standing quietly with her ear to the opening, she listened, picking up snippets of conversation: "disk," "more money," "do as I say," "where's my mother?," "shoot," "gun." *Gun?* What was going on down there? She had better remain quiet until she knew more.

A slight pain was beginning in the center of her chest, and she went over to where her purse lay on the nightstand. John must have placed it there. Digging for her medication, she came across everything *but*: wallet, comb, compact, lipstick, nail file. No pills. Great! Then she remembered. She had taken the medicine before rushing out with John and had left the bottle by the kitchen sink. A lot of good it'll do there!

Her upset over the entire situation worsened the pain.

Suddenly, a crash came from downstairs. Dropping the purse on the bed, she rushed to the door.

CHAPTER FORTY-SIX

SLADE'S HEART WAS BEATING SO HARD HE THOUGHT IT WOULD burst through his chest. His resolve began to melt as he watched John thrust both the tray he proffered and the gun to within an inch of Stasi's face. What had he gotten her into? If he hadn't needed her to drive, he would never have allowed her to come. Now here she was, being forced to down a lethal drink. Droplets formed on his forehead as he practically willed Stasi not to accept the drink. His breath caught in his throat when her hand rose up toward the tray, but what she did next was totally unexpected.

In one swift movement, Stasi swung her arm in an arc, and before Slade knew what was happening, the tray and the two drinks had flown across the room and crashed to the floor.

"You dirty little . . .!" John shouted and backhanded Stasi across the face. The impact of the blow caused her to shriek, and, resembling a ragdoll, her body flopped sideways into the cushions of the sofa.

Slade charged like a raging bull, propelling himself off the sofa with surprising agility and catching John around the waist. The thick carpet broke their fall, but John lost his grip on the gun, which bounced out of his hand and out of his reach.

They grappled together on the floor for several minutes, but because John had the use of his legs and Slade didn't, John was able to wrench himself free and spring for the gun. Stasi hoisted herself from the sofa and lunged at John, landing on his back piggyback fashion. Before he could grasp the gun, she pummeled his head with one hand while covering his eyes with the other so that he groped around like a blind man. Finally, he seized both her hands, bent over, and flipped her, then thrust her aside with so much force that she fell against the entertainment center, bumping her head on its corner and collapsing to the floor.

When Slade saw Stasi lying still and a drop of blood trickling from her temple, he immediately wanted to go to her, but he knew it was more important to deal with John first. Otherwise, none of them would get out of there alive.

To distract John until he could make his way over to him, Slade grabbed ashtrays and other decorative pieces from the tables, throwing them at John and dragging himself forward at the same time. John covered his head with his arms and dropped to the floor, inching his way toward the gun.

Slade was almost upon him, but he needed a few more crucial seconds. Taking a large, flat crystal ashtray, he placed it on the floor, pushing it with all his might to slide it across the carpet in a direct path to the gun. The ashtray whizzed toward the gun but slowed as it approached, nudging the gun only a few inches farther away from John. This wasn't the effect Slade was hoping for, but he'd do the best he could with what he had.

Finally close enough, Slade reached out and took John's ankles in a vise-like grip. Using all the strength in his powerful arms, he yanked John toward him. Just in time, for John had almost had the gun in his hand!

Slade threw himself on top of John and wrestled with him, wondering all the while how he was going to stop him. He got in a few good punches, but so did John. Then John swung his left fist, catching Slade between the eyes with such force that he could barely focus, and Slade slumped slightly forward. John seized the opportunity by pushing Slade off and switching their positions so that he was sitting on Slade's abdomen. He swung a few more punches into Slade's face until finally Slade sank into deep, dark oblivion.

CHAPTER FORTY-SEVEN

THIS WAS TOO MUCH TO TAKE! LOIS HEARD TERRIBLE THINGS going on down there: crashing, Stasi screaming, Slade yelling, John yelling. She didn't know the circumstances, but she wished she could do something. If only she could get out of this room!

She glanced around for something she could use to break that chain. No good. Nothing. Going over to the door, she tried to use her fingers to push the chain out of the glider, but her arm would get crushed in the door before she could slide the chain to the end of the slot. Nevertheless, she tried and tried, even to the point that a piece of her fingernail was broken off.

Walking over to the bed, she flounced down on it in a huff. Praying for a solution, she picked up the nail file she had dumped out of her purse earlier and began idly filing the broken fingernail.

It came to her so suddenly she barely realized it. The nail file might work!

Hurrying over to the door, she opened it just far enough to fit her hand through and began working the chain.

CHAPTER FORTY-EIGHT

JOHN STOOD OVER SLADE WITH THE GUN POISED. HE WASN'T sure he had it in him to shoot someone point-blank. If he was *forced* to do it, he could. But then, looking at the two young people sprawled in various positions around the room, he figured that since they were already unconscious, he would simply burn the house down.

Wistfully, John's gaze glided around the large living room of the cabin. He hated to ruin this beautiful place. There were some wonderful memories made here, and he was going to miss it. Shrugging his shoulders, he suppressed that thought. *Oh, well, I won't be needing a cabin where* I'm *going*. He chuckled quietly as he headed to the back of the house and into the yard, then to the shed where he kept a can of gasoline.

Lois crept down the stairs, trying to ignore the crushing pain in her chest. At the bottom of the steps, she came to an abrupt stop at the sight of John brushing some imaginary lint from his suit before bending to pick up a gun. She frowned and shook her head, unable to comprehend what she was seeing.

Barely able to suppress a loud gasp, Lois moved to conceal herself behind a nearby wall as she watched John point the gun at her son. Then, miraculously, he lowered his arm, gazed around the room admiringly, slipped the gun into a side pocket of his suit jacket, and with a toothy grin strode from the room.

Clutching her chest, Lois stumbled over to Slade. Dropping to her knees, she checked him over and almost cried out at the sight of his swollen, bloodied face. "Slade!" she whispered loudly. "Get up!" He didn't budge. She moaned inwardly and put her ear to his chest. His heart was still beating strong.

She didn't have time for anything else, because she heard a door at the back of the house opening. Rushing back to the wall where she had first hidden, she watched in silence.

John whistled as he unscrewed the cap to a gasoline can and flung it aside, then proceeded to sprinkle the contents over the carpet. Lois trembled at the sight of this, realizing what he meant to do. It was up to her to do something now. Offering a small prayer, she turned from the wall and moved down the short hall that led to the large, open kitchen. Trying to be as quiet as possible, she opened one of the drawers. Knives! She would stay away from *them*. She couldn't even entertain the thought of handling one in these circumstances. She tried another drawer, but about a third of the way open it began to creak, so she left it. Trying a lower cabinet, she came across some pots and pans. The pain in her chest was becoming unbearable, but she had to keep going for Slade and Stasi. Crouching down to peer in, the cabinet was dark, and she could hardly see, but she stuck her hand in to feel around. Coming across something heavy, she pulled it out to find a cast-iron skillet. *Perfect*! She hurried back toward the living room.

The gasoline can was no longer in sight, and the front door was wide open. John was fumbling with something in his hand, and the expression on his face showed anger and frustration. Lois's eye caught the glint of metal, and she realized that it was a lighter and that John was angry because it was giving him trouble.

What should she do? If she went right up to him, he'd wrestle the pan from her, or worse. He *did* have a gun. She needed to get behind him. Ignoring the chest pain, she headed back toward the kitchen and came out through the back door, thankful that this huge cabin had so many exits.

It was light outside, and Lois easily found her way around to the front of the house. Approaching the steps to the porch, she quietly made her way up and peeked in through the door. John stood about eight feet away from her, facing the opposite way. She guessed he intended to light the fire and escape through the front door.

Slowly and quietly, she tiptoed toward him. Coming up close, she raised the cumbrous pan high and swung sideways with all her might, catching John on the side of the head. He must have sensed her behind him, because he was in a quarter turn when she hit him.

In what seemed like slow motion, John turned fully and glanced at her, dazed, stumbling back a few paces as his limp hand released the now lit lighter.

As John's body made contact with the floor, so did the lighter, and Lois watched in horror as the fire was ignited.

CHAPTER FORTY-NINE

SOMEONE WAS SLAPPING HIS FACE, AND HE HEARD A FAMILIAR faraway voice screaming his name. He felt hot. Opening his eyes, he saw a blurred form looming over him. Where was he? Slowly his memory returned. *John's cabin, John's deceit, John kidnapping his mother.*

Gradually, his eyes became focused, and he saw his mother hovering over him. Relief overtook him, and he reached up and snatched her to him in a bear hug, tumbling her on top of him. "Mom! Thank goodness you're safe!"

Lois fought against him, and her screams were muffled into his chest. "What is it?" He let her go and suddenly became aware of an infernal heat and the odor of something burning.

Lois sat up. "Are you crazy? We have to get out of here! John set the house on fire!"

"What! Where's Stasi?"

"Over there." She pointed across the room where Stasi was beginning to stir and moan.

"Help me get her out," he yelled as he proceeded to drag himself forward. Then he noticed Lois holding her chest and the pained expression on her face and added, "Stasi has your medicine in her pocket. Take it when you get out."

Reaching Stasi, Slade sat by her and lifted her shoulders up until she was in a sitting position. He gently patted her cheeks, saying, "C'mon, sweetie, wake up!" She barely had her eyes open. "Can you stand up? There's a fire! We have to get out!"

Stasi nodded and coughed, for the smoke had permeated the room. Lois helped Stasi to her feet and held onto her as she hobbled toward the door on her precarious limbs. Slade dragged himself behind but stopped when he saw John sprawled out on the floor.

"Mom!" he yelled, and when both she and Stasi stopped and turned toward him, he jerked his head in John's direction. "What happened?"

"I hit him with a cast-iron skillet," she yelled back over the roar of the fire. "Come on, Slade! We haven't much time!" Then she turned Stasi about and continued toward the door.

Slade didn't move. He cringed as a curio cabinet was disintegrated by flames and fell so close to him he could reach out and touch the burning object. Other furniture was beginning to do the same.

He looked toward the door, then back at John. Should he leave him? After all, John *did* try to kill him. More than once.

He started toward the door, then stopped. He couldn't just leave him here to die.

"I'm going to help him!" he yelled to his mother and Stasi, who had just reached the door. "You two go!"

"No!" they screamed in unison.

He waved his arm for them to keep going, then dragged himself toward John. When he reached him, he noticed a thin stream of blood oozing from the side of his head. He began slapping at his face, but John didn't budge. He shook John's shoulders. "John! C'mon, wake up!" Still no response, and time was running out. The flames had spread across the path to the door, but they were small. John must have been running out of gasoline by the time he got to that area.

Looking around, Slade spotted two throws draped over the back of the sofa and the loveseat. Dragging himself over seemed to take forever, but he made it and yanked both throws off and made his way back to John. He wrapped John completely with the larger throw and covered his own head and shoulders with the smaller one, leaving his arms free.

Now came the hard part. In a sitting position at John's feet, he grasped John's ankles through the coverlet and yanked them toward himself. Then, using the floor for leverage, he pushed himself backwards with his hands. He repeated this process over and over as he inched himself and John toward the door.

Approaching the flames in their path, Slade could see that they were as high as his shoulders. Using the same process, he plowed on, taking himself and John through the flames as fast as he could. Twice during the journey, his hands and forearms caught fire, but he quickly snuffed the flames out with the heavy coverlet. John's throw was now covered in flames, so Slade knew his must be, too. The two men would roll on the ground when they got outside. No matter how painful it was using his burnt hands or how much his lungs hurt from smoke inhalation, he kept moving.

Exhausted, Slade labored to pull himself and John through the door. He heard sirens and some vehicles screeching to a halt behind him, then several thuds of car doors and people shouting. Finally, he felt many strong hands carrying him down the porch steps and onto the grass, where he was rolled over to snuff the flames.

Stasi and Lois immediately attached themselves to him, crying, but paramedics waved them away and began working on him.

The cold mountain air felt good on his parched face, and the oxygen being administered relieved his lungs. Wondering how John was, he peered between all the people fussing over him to get a glimpse. John had an oxygen mask over his face, and he seemed to be coming around.

Within seconds, Slade succumbed to his exhaustion, and all went black.

Slade opened his eyes to a view of Stasi asleep in a chair next to the hospital bed. Aside from the bandage on her temple, the very sight brought to mind another time when she'd always been there beside him at the hospital. What had he done to deserve her?

Actually, nothing. He'd treated her badly back then. Why she wasted all that time with him, he had no idea. One thing he *did* know was that he loved her. She was everything to him. If it hadn't been for her, he would never have gotten his life on the right track. He'd never have found his Lord. The plus was that these past months with her were the happiest he'd ever experienced. Even in a wheelchair.

If only he could spend the rest of his life with her. Marry her. But he couldn't. He wouldn't. His dependency would be too much of a burden. She deserved a *real* man. Someone who could protect her and take care of her. He was none of those things.

He heard a rustle from the opposite corner of the room. He turned and saw his mother pushing herself out of a chair, rubbing her eyes. As she came to stand by the bed, she placed a finger against her lips. "Don't wake her," she whispered, inclining her head in Stasi's direction. "She needs the rest. She wouldn't stay in her own room."

Slade nodded, not wanting to speak anyway. His gaze returned to Stasi.

"You love her, don't you?"

He looked at his mother, not surprised that she knew. Anyone could tell, he supposed. He hadn't realized until now how transparent he was in that area. "Yes."

Lois patted his hand. "That's good."

He shook his head.

"Why not?" she whispered loudly, her ire up.

Slade glanced at Stasi to make sure she hadn't heard his mother's outburst. She hadn't budged. "She deserves better."

She pushed his hair back off his forehead. "Not because you're my son, but who could be better? You're honest, kind, gentle. . ."

"You know what I mean, Mom."

She nodded. "I guess I do." After a brief pause, "Stasi told me you're saved now. Maybe you should pray about it before you make any rash decisions."

Slade looked at her. He hadn't thought of that.

Slade was going home later today. Aside from some minor burns on his hands and forearms, he was fine, but they had kept him overnight at the hospital. John too. Right now, Slade was using his bandaged hands to wheel his way down the hall to where he was told John's room was. Without knowing why, he had a strong urge to see John before leaving.

Arriving at the door to John's room, he stopped, hesitated, then rolled past the police guard and into the room. John appeared to be asleep, so Slade began to whirl his chair around to leave.

"Slade." John's voice was weak.

Slade stopped and turned back. John's head was bandaged where Lois had hit him with the skillet. His face pale and wan. Slade didn't move, however, but stayed and waited.

"I'm glad you came."

Slade shrugged. Now that he was here, he wasn't sure what to say to the man who had wanted him dead.

"I think your mother knocked some sense into me."

Slade smiled faintly.

"How do you feel?" John asked him.

"Aside from the pain of my burnt hands?" he asked, holding up two bandaged stumps.

Turning his head away, John mumbled, "Sorry about that."

Slade remained quiet.

"I was told that it was you who saved my life," John said, turning back again.

Slade nodded.

"Why, after everything I've done to you?"

Slade shook his head. "I don't know. I almost didn't, but in the end, I couldn't just leave you there."

"Thank you," John said, sounding like he meant it. "I'm grateful for the choice you made."

"Only my conscience kept me from leaving you."

John nodded. "I would have deserved it if you had."

Slade just shrugged, feeling awkward. What do you say to someone who has tried to kill you? But he was amazed at what John said next, and he knew he had to answer.

"Slade, can you ever forgive me? I never meant to let things get so out of hand."

Never had Slade thought he could feel so tranquil at such an intense moment. John seemed truly remorseful, and Slade's heart was wide open. He breathed a contented sigh. "Yes, John, I forgive you."

John gave him a weak smile, which Slade returned. Then he spun his chair and rolled out of the room.

Feeling light and free, Slade knew that now he could live peaceably. Everything had fallen into place, and he could get on with his life. And he was sure that he would really start living for the first time.

CHAPTER FIFTY

SLADE WAS NERVOUS. STASI WOULD BE OVER ANY second. Strangely enough, she had called him on the phone to say she wanted to talk to him about something important. Normally, she would have just come right on over without warning. But that's not why he was jittery. It was that he wanted to talk to her, too. About something *very* important.

Sitting in his wheelchair beside the sofa, he jumped at the sound of the doorknob turning. He spun the chair around to see Stasi slowly closing the door. She stood for a moment, leaning her forehead against the door, not facing him, as if she weren't ready to.

"Stasi?"

She turned, this time leaning her back against the door. He could sense her apprehensiveness. It seemed that he wasn't the only one who was nervous.

She walked toward him, wringing her hands. "Hi, Slade."

"Hello." He extended one of his still bandaged hands, his fingers now free. Taking it, she held onto it as she walked around him and seated herself on the couch beside his chair. He looked at her, sitting with her head down, hands clamped between her knees. With what little of his fingers were now exposed, he couldn't resist touching the wisps that had escaped the claw-clip where her dark hair was caught up on top of her head. He knew they'd be soft. *She* looked soft, too, in her faded jeans and fuzzy yellow sweater.

Finally looking up, she said, "It seems strange not having Lois around."

Lois was supposed to have stayed until after New Year's, but she had flown home the day before, saying she needed a vacation from her vacation. "Yes, it does, but we'll see her again soon. Maybe fly down to Florida in the spring." He watched her reaction hopefully.

Her sapphire gaze rested on him and softened. "That would be lovely."

He was getting impatient, and curiosity got the best of him. "What did you want to talk to me about?"

Growing fidgety, she wrung her hands again, stood up, and began pacing around the room. "I don't really know how to say this, except to just plunge right in." Except she faltered instead of plunging. "I . . .I think. . ." She turned her back to him, facing the window.

"What, Stasi? What is it?"

"I think we should get married, Slade. I'm asking because I love you, and I know you love me, but I also know you wouldn't ask me because you think you're not a whole man. You're more of a man than anyone I know, and I think I should have a say in the matter. I don't think you should deny me my happiness just because *you* think I deserve better . . ."

She stopped, as if she suddenly realized she was rambling, but she still wouldn't face him. He wheeled over to within two feet of where she stood. "Stasi, look at me."

"Why can't you believe that it doesn't matter?" she began as she turned to face him. Then she stopped, her features softening into an understanding smile.

He sat gazing up at her, feeling the wide grin on his face. He wasn't denying anything she had just said. As a matter of fact, marriage was the very subject he had intended to broach himself. "You don't need to convince me anymore."

Eyes wide, her jaw dropped. "You mean . . .?"

"Yes. And now, *I'm* asking *you*: Will you marry me?"

The changing expressions that marched across her face showed him she was at first surprised, then ecstatic.

"Oh, Slade!" She knelt at the side of the wheelchair. "Yes!" Throwing her arms around his neck, she added, "I love you!"

Serious now, he nudged her arms from around his neck and stared deep into her eyes. "And I love you, Stasi. I have for a long time, but I just didn't want to admit it to you. I thought that once I acknowledged it, it would be too painful to endure, thinking I could never have you."

"And I would have waited for you forever," she whispered, blinking away unshed tears.

They gazed into each other's eyes for a few moments more, conveying without words all they held within their hearts. Then Stasi broke the spell.

"Enough mooning! We have to celebrate! We have to call your mother! But first," she climbed onto his lap, "give me a ride!"

Slade laughed as her arms encircled his neck. "You're crazy, you know that?" he said affectionately.

"Yeah. Crazy about you." She planted a smacking kiss on his lips.

They both laughed as Slade's bandaged hands awkwardly maneuvered the wheelchair into a dance of spins, circles, and wheelies.